'You're a romantic, Dr Bailey?'

Brooke smiled at Matt before returning her gaze to the couple in front of them. 'And a dreamer. But don't we all hope and dream for happiness in some way?'

Matt didn't answer. But he stared at her profile, at the way her nose turned up slightly at the end, at the fullness of her smiling lips, at the gentle way one brown tress of hair had escaped her messy bun and rested upon her shoulder. It looked soft and silky, and it seemed wrong to him that someone as sweet and lovely as her should be alone when clearly she had so much love to give.

He concentrated for a moment on his notes. Blood pressure. Respirations. Pulse. Patient. But his mind wouldn't stay focused. It was as if there was a small cyclone of thoughts whizzing around, picking up the leaves of his thoughts and tossing them into the mix.

Lily.

Yes. His daughter had to be his priority. Worrying about Brooke's love life was not his responsibility. Nothing to do with him. She was his friend, but that was all she would ever be. He couldn't allow himself to think any more of her than that.

But if that was the case then why was she the only thing he could think about?

Dear Reader,

When I had my babies I went to a variety of baby classes. One of them was a Music and Movement class, where I naively thought that I'd get to sit on the floor holding my baby and helping her move to music—kind of like baby yoga.

Only it wasn't a class where I could sit on my butt and pretend my baby was enjoying herself. It was a singing and dancing class, and the leader announced at the first one that we would *'all go round the circle, take it in turns to dance into the centre, and introduce yourself and your baby!'*

I'm sure you can imagine my horror.

So I had to include something similar in Brooke and Matt's story. It was hilarious revisiting all those old feelings and memories and the cringe-worthy stuff you put yourself through in an effort to be a good parent.

Brooke and Matt are trying to be excellent parents. They want to do what's best for their babies, no matter how strong their urge to stay indoors and hibernate away from the rest of the world. They learn, as we all do, that some days you just have to push through.

I hope you enjoy reading their story as much as I enjoyed writing it.

Love,

Louisa xx

THEIR DOUBLE BABY GIFT

BY
LOUISA HEATON

HarperCollins
P U B L I S H E R S
Since

RF

Published in Great Britain 2017
By Mills & Boon, an imprint of HarperCollins*Publishers*
1 London Bridge Street, London, SE1 9GF

© 2017 Louisa Heaton

ISBN: 978-0-263-06939-6

Printed and bound in Great Britain
by CPI Antony Rowe, Chippenham, Wiltshire

Louisa Heaton lives on Hayling Island, Hampshire, with her husband, four children and a small zoo. She has worked in various roles in the health industry—most recently four years as a Community First Responder, answering 999 calls. When not writing Louisa enjoys other creative pursuits, including reading, quilting and patchwork—usually instead of the things she *ought* to be doing!

Books by Louisa Heaton

Mills & Boon Medical Romance

The Baby That Changed Her Life
His Perfect Bride?
A Father This Christmas?
One Life-Changing Night
Seven Nights with Her Ex
Christmas with the Single Dad
Reunited by Their Pregnancy Surprise

Visit the Author Profile page
at millsandboon.co.uk for more titles.

For Becca xxx

**Praise for
Louisa Heaton**

'An emotional rollercoaster ride… *One Life-Changing Night* is medical drama at its best.'

CHAPTER ONE

SHE WAS RUNNING LATE. *Very* late. And as she stared at the clock on the car dashboard it seemed to be whizzing through minutes, as if a mischievous imp was maniacally pressing down hard on the fast-forward button.

Why was this happening *today?* Today of all days? Her first day back after maternity leave. Her first day as a single working mother, back in the A&E department she loved. A department that would now be all the quieter because Jen wasn't in it.

Dr Brooke Bailey had *so* wanted this day to start well. Because if it did—if she got through it—then that would be all the proof she needed that her decision to do this on her own was a good one.

It had seemed doable in the early months of her pregnancy, when bravado and optimism had got her through the days. She didn't need a man. She didn't need anyone. Only herself—which was just as well, seeing as there wasn't a whole lot of people she could turn to now. Millions of other single mothers held down a job and coped, didn't they? Why should it be any more difficult for *her*?

Only back then, with her rose-tinted spectacles on, she hadn't predicted that she'd be awake the night before going back to work, doing hourly feeds because Morgan wouldn't settle. She hadn't expected that the very second she'd decided to strap Morgan into the car for her commute to work Morgan would have an almighty nappy explosion and would need to be taken back inside the house to be bathed and have everything changed.

Nor had she forecast that she would get caught in an endless traffic jam, tapping her fingers impatiently on the wheel as she glanced at the London Grace Hospital—so temptingly close, but unattainable—as she sat bumper to bumper between a four-wheel drive and a large white delivery van, listening to people sounding their horns. She was wincing with each one, hoping that the noise wouldn't wake her daughter, who was finally—thankfully—asleep.

Beside her on the passenger seat her mobile phone trilled with a message, and as the traffic wasn't moving she decided to check her hands-free device.

It was Kelly.

Where are you? X

She couldn't respond. Not behind the wheel. Even if she *was* stuck in traffic. She'd seen enough evidence of what happened to people when they drove and texted. The cars might move at any moment. She could be texting and have someone rear-end her and give her whiplash as well as a late mark for her first day.

Not only had she to find a space and park the car, she also had to get Morgan to the hospital crèche.

An event she'd been worrying about for weeks.

It had seemed such a simple thing when she'd first planned it—*I'll just put the baby in the crèche.* But what if her baby didn't like it? What if she screamed the place down? What if she clung to her mother and refused to let go?

She'd never left Morgan alone with a *friend*, let alone in a crèche for ten hours a day. Eric had seen to it that she'd lost touch with most of her friends. Had isolated her until no one was left. So that when she had walked away, when she had broken free, she'd felt so ashamed about what she'd allowed to happen she'd felt she couldn't call anyone.

It had just been her and Morgan. And that had been enough. Till now.

Snakes of anticipation coiled in her stomach at the thought of leaving her daughter, and she was just contemplating sounding her own horn when the traffic finally began to move and she could make the turning into the hospital car park. Free, she zoomed up to the barrier, wound down her window to let in the mixed aroma of exhaust fumes and recent rain, swiped her card over the scanner and watched the barrier slowly rise.

For the first time ever she could take advantage of the parent and child spaces on the ground floor near the lift, and she pulled into an empty space. 'Thank you, thank you, thank you...' she muttered to any car park god there might be, and got out of the car, opening up the boot to assemble the buggy.

She got Morgan into it in record time, and without tears, and headed on over to the lift.

As the lift slowly took her up to the floor she needed she contemplated what it would be like to work a shift without Jen.

Jen had been a recent friend. But an amazing one. An unexpected treasure Brooke had located when she'd first started working at the London Grace. At the time she had still been with Eric, but she'd been having serious doubts, starting to be sure that she would have to walk away from him, but struggling with her conscience about the best way to do it with her pride still intact.

Her mood had been low and pensive as she'd stood in the staff room one day, dunking a tea bag over and over. In had walked a woman with a bright streak of pink in her short blonde hair—a shade of pink that had matched the stethoscope draped around her neck.

She'd taken one look at Brooke, walked right up to her, put her arm around Brooke's shoulder and said, *'Whoever he is, dump him. No man should make you look like that!'*

It had been the beginning of a beautiful friendship, and when Brooke had dumped Eric, and then found out a few weeks later that she was pregnant and Eric wanted nothing to do with her or the baby, Jen had been the one who had picked her up, dusted her down and taken her to a show where there'd been masses of gyrating male strippers and lots and lots of hot, writhing, perfectly muscled flesh.

Brooke smiled as she recalled that night. Jen had been an absolute diamond. Rough-cut, maybe, but still one of a kind. And when Jen had discovered that she too was pregnant, and that they had due dates within days of each other that had just solidified their friendship all the more.

Jen's husband Matt had been in the army medical corps, and hardly ever at home, so she and Jen had grown their babies together, comparing bump sizes and ankle swellings and seeing who could hold their pee the longest before having to wobble off to the bathroom.

But I don't have Jen to pick me up any more. No one to pick me up if the day turns out to be the biggest mistake of my entire life.

As the lift pinged open and Brooke began striding down the long corridor that would take her to the hospital crèche she tried not to go over that phone call once again. When Kelly had called to let her know that Jen had died during the birth—complications from eclampsia.

At the time she herself had just delivered Morgan. Had been home for just three days and struggling to get her daughter to latch on. Frustration had been building and the sound of the phone had been a welcome distraction. A few moments to gather herself and calm down. Contact from the outside world.

And then...

She swallowed back tears. She could not cry today. It was stressful enough without going over Jen's death all the time. Life moved on. You couldn't stop its inexorable march. Jen was dead. Brooke was alone. *Again.* She was back at work. Late. She needed to get a move on or she'd have a cranky boss to deal with too.

She buzzed at the door and a staff member let her in.

'I've brought Morgan Bailey. It's her first day...' She tried to sound braver and more together than she really felt.

The crèche nurse wore a bright tabard decorated in a multitude of teddy bears, with a name badge that said *'Daisy'*. Like the flower, she seemed bright and sunny, as if her face had a permanent smile upon it.

Behind her, Brooke could see children playing in a small ball pit, others daubing painted handprints onto a long strip of what looked like wallpaper, others at a table drawing, another group listening to a story. Beyond was another door, labelled *'Baby Room'*, and as she looked the door opened and a tall man with a military demeanour stepped out.

But she had no time to concentrate on him—despite the fact that some tired, exhausted part of her sex-starved brain still worked and had registered how attractive he was. The bossier part of her brain—the exhausted, sleep-deprived, worried-about-being-late part—overrode all other messages.

She unbuckled Morgan from the buggy and lifted her out. 'She's been up most of the night, I'm afraid, so she might be a little grumpy. There are bottles in the bag…' she unhooked the baby bag from the handles of the buggy and handed it over '…with expressed milk. I've labelled them with her name, so you can give her the right ones. There's a teddy in the bag, that's her favourite—Mr Cuddles. She likes to sleep with it. You usually have to wind her twice before she'll go to sleep, and if you sing her *"Baa-Baa Black Sheep"* she'll cry, so please don't do that. And…and…'

She couldn't help it. The tears that had been stinging the backs of her eyes now readily began to fall. The moment of having to hand her daughter over was too much. Her little girl had been the one to keep her together these past few months. She was all she had, and now…

Morgan, sensing her mother's distress, began to cry, and now Brooke was feeling worse about leaving her baby. She stood there clutching her daughter, hiccupping her way through her own tears, as if giving her up to the crèche meant certain death.

I can't do this! I don't need to work, do I? I could wait a little longer, take some more time off. I—

Daisy reached forward to take the crying Morgan. 'We'll be fine—don't worry. Have you got the crèche app on your phone?'

The hospital crèche had developed its own app, so that parents could click in at any time during the day and receive updates about their child—whether they'd slept, when they'd eaten or had a bottle, what the child was playing with. There was even an option to access the crèche's webcam.

Grateful for the fact that Daisy was ignoring Brooke's embarrassing tears, she tried to breathe. Sucking in a breath and dragging a tissue from her pocket to wipe her nose, Brooke nodded. 'Yes.'

Daisy was still smiling and bobbing up and down as she gently swayed Morgan, trying to soothe her. 'You go off to work, then, Mummy. Don't worry about us.'

Morgan looked sickeningly distressed to be in a stranger's arms, which was disconcerting for her mother. 'I've never left her before. You'll call me if there's any problem?'

'Of course we will.'

'Anything at all?'

Daisy nodded, but as Brooke opened her mouth to ask another question she felt a firm hand upon her arm. The man she'd seen before looked down at her with intense blue eyes and said, 'It's best to just walk away. Don't look back.'

Brooke looked up at him hopefully, gratefully, with her ugly crying face still at full throttle, dabbing at her tears and trying to hold on to his words of wisdom. Had he done this, then? Did he know what he was talking about? He'd just come out of the Baby Room, so perhaps he'd just dropped off his own child?

'Really?'

'Really. Come on.'

He had a stern, no-nonsense tone to his voice. A voice that was used to issuing commands and having them obeyed without question. It was clear he expected the same from her. He gently draped his hands over hers, forcing her fingers to release the death grip she'd had on the buggy since letting go of her daughter, then took the buggy from her and parked it in the buggy bay. With a guiding hand in the small of her back, he purposefully escorted her to the exit.

Brooke was desperate to turn around and make sure Morgan was okay. She could still hear her baby wailing. Her daughter *needed* her. But the man blocked her view and ushered her out through the door and into the corridor like an expert collie dog herding a reluctant sheep.

'But I need to—'

He held up his hand for silence. 'No. You don't.'

Brooke stepped away and looked him up and down, irritated that he thought he knew what she needed. Sniffing desperately and wiping her nose with the tissue, she wondered just who this man was, anyway. She'd never seen him before at the hospital. But, then again, she'd never had reason to come to the crèche before and the hospital was a big place. He might work anywhere. He might be a new employee.

Wiping away the last of her tears, she stared up at him. He was a good head taller than she. With very short dark blond hair, longer on top. Piercing blue eyes. Trim. Oozing strength and quiet, confident dominance. That was something that usually rubbed her up the wrong way. Eric had been overbearing. Had tried to control her. It was the kind of thing to send up the warning flags.

'Look, I appreciate that you're trying to help me, but—'

'If they sense weakness it makes them more upset.'

She wiped her nose again for good measure, sure it was now probably as red as strawberry jelly. 'The babies?'

He gave one curt nod.

'She's five months old. The only thing she senses is hunger, tiredness and whether she's wet or not.'

'You'd be surprised.' He began to walk away.

Narrowing her eyes, Brooke followed after him. He was going in her direction anyway. She needed the lift again, to go down a couple of floors to A&E.

She pulled her mobile from her pocket to check the time.

Damn it!

The man got into the lift ahead of her. 'Which floor?'

'Ground level.' She noticed he'd pressed the 'G' button, but no other. Frowning, she realised that he must work on her floor. He might work anywhere, though—A&E, the Medical Assessment Unit, Nuclear Medicine, Radiology…

He was looking at her. Looking her up and down. And, sickeningly, she noticed his gaze appeared to be centred on her chest. *Men!* Feeling her cheeks heat, she stared back at him, trying to make him lift his gaze a good few inches upwards, towards her face.

'Is there a problem?'

'You…er…might want to get out of those clothes.'

'Excuse me?' He had some front! He'd only just met her!

What is it with men? They do you one tiny favour and suddenly expect you to drop your—

'You've got milk on your blouse, something questionable on your skirt, and you appear to be…' he smiled and looked away, as if he was preserving her modesty '…leaking.'

Leaking? Brooke looked down at herself and instantly felt her cheeks flame with heat. She was indeed in a state. Her boobs *had* leaked milk—no doubt due to Morgan's cries—she had a smear of what might possibly be poo at the top of her thigh from the earlier explosion, and there was indeed a smelly, sour milk stain, crusting away on her shoulder.

'Oh, God…'

She reached into her handbag for wipes, but she didn't have any. They were all in the nappy bag that she'd left with Daisy down in the crèche. She couldn't work looking like this! She'd have to put some scrubs on. Making her even more late!

The lift doors pinged open and both she and the military man stepped out and turned left towards A&E. Frowning, Brooke looked at him once again, noting his proud bearing, his *march* rather than stride, and the fact that they were both most definitely heading towards the same department.

'Do you work in A&E?' she asked, curious.

Had she embarrassed herself in front of a new work colleague? Staff did come and go frequently. It was a pressured environment—stressful. Some people couldn't hack it. But Brooke could. She loved it there.

'I do.'

'I work there, too.'

He stopped in his tracks immediately and looked at her, this time with a single raised eyebrow. 'This is your first day back after maternity leave?'

How did he know that? Unless her friends had mentioned it to him… 'Yes.'

His eyes widened. '*You're* Dr Bailey?'

She nodded, surprised that he knew her name. 'Yes. Who are *you*?'

He didn't answer right away, and it took him a moment before he held out his hand. 'Major Matt Galloway. Jen's husband.'

She was unaware that her mouth had dropped open. But she numbly reached forward and shook his hand anyway.

She'd meant to call. She'd *meant* to. Only… Life had

got in the way and she'd been struggling to cope herself. Life was harder and busier than she'd suspected it would be with a baby, and she was doing everything alone. Jen's death three days after she'd given birth to Morgan had made her postnatal blues a lot worse and she'd been grieving herself.

Trying to get herself together just to get dressed and out of the house had seemed an insurmountable task— and then there was the fact that she'd never met Jen's husband. She'd thought it might be awkward if she just turned up at their house on the other side of London. So she'd put it off and put it off, and when finally she'd thought that she really ought to go and offer her condolences and help so much time had passed she'd just felt that it wouldn't be right.

It had made her feel incredibly guilty, and now the last person she'd expected to run into at work was Jen's widower.

Had he just dropped off Lily?

She hadn't even been able to make it to Jen's funeral on time. She'd misjudged how long it would take her to get ready and out of the house, and when she'd got there the funeral had already started. She'd slipped into the back of the church and huddled in a pew at the back. Then—naturally—Morgan had begun crying and, not wishing to disturb the service, she'd crept back out. The only thing that would settle her daughter was being pushed in her pram, so she'd gone for a walk.

Returning to the church long after the service had finished she had stood looking down at Jen's grave, tears dripping down her cheeks. Feeling *so* alone.

She'd thought maybe that Jen would have forgiven her for being late. It was the kind of person she'd been.

But Matt...? She had no idea how he'd feel. All she

knew from Jen was that he was a stickler for rules and regulations.

'Erm…hello.' She managed a smile, aware now that he had seen her at her worst. 'I didn't expect to see you here.'

'I work here.'

He did?

'I've taken up Jen's post. I needed to be working after—' He stopped talking suddenly, his eyes darkening, and looked away.

'I'm so sorry for your loss. I did make it to the funeral. And I tried to stay, but…'

'But your baby started to cry and you took her outside.'

'You noticed?'

He nodded, looking at her strangely. 'I heard.'

'I tried to make it back, but by the time she'd settled you'd all gone.'

'That's okay. I imagine you had your hands full.'

'Well, I'm sure you did, too. How *are* things with the baby? It's Lily, isn't it?'

'Yes. They're difficult. She's teething. Not sleeping very well.'

Morgan had just started teething too, so Brooke knew the misery of that. 'It gets easier, they say. Let's hang on to that.'

He continued to look at her carefully. 'We should show our faces, seeing as we're both late.'

She nodded. 'Yes—yes, you're right. Don't want to anger the boss on the first day.'

'You haven't angered me.'

Brooke blinked. '*You're* my boss?'

'I'm Clinical Lead, yes.'

'Right…'

She wasn't sure what to say to that. The department had obviously gone through some changes she didn't know about. Why hadn't Kelly let her know? She'd mentioned they'd got some new eye candy in charge, but hadn't mentioned who he was. Why not?

'Well, I'm sorry I'm late.'

'Why don't you get changed and meet me in my office in ten minutes? There are a few new protocols you need to be aware of, and then I'll assign you your duties.'

'Sure.' She nodded and smiled as he marched off towards his office.

Her new boss.

Jen's *husband*.

She looked upwards, as if to heaven, and muttered, 'You had to throw me one last curveball, huh?'

She shook her head in disbelief and pictured Jen grinning down at her.

Her first patient was a guy in his forties. When she called his name in the waiting room he stood up, one hand supporting the other. His triage card said *'Query fracture left wrist'*.

Matt had assigned her to Minors. She'd gone to the changing room, got into a pair of dark blue scrubs. When she'd gone to put her own clothes into her locker she'd done a double-take, noticing that Jen's locker was just as she'd left it. No one had cleared it out yet. Seeing it there, with her friend's name still on it, plastered with pictures of Hollywood heartthrobs, had made her heart miss a beat. In a way she was glad that no one had rushed to empty it. It meant that Jen had been valued. Loved.

Brooke had scooped her long brown hair up into a messy bun and set off to see Matt.

He'd looked every inch an army officer, seated behind his desk with his straight back in his neat office, everything perfectly positioned and aligned. He'd clasped his hands on the desk in front of him and run her through the new burns protocols and triage assessments.

Sitting there, looking at him, she'd wondered if the reason he held himself so formally in check was because he might fall apart if he relaxed. He seemed very stiff and distant now he was working—nothing like his relaxed, friendly, affable wife, who'd thought nothing of draping her arms around the shoulders of friends, who'd positively warmed everyone with her wide smile and closeness.

And then he'd said, 'When you've dealt with each of your patients I'd like you to run your results past me before you discharge anyone.'

Run her results past him?

'Why?'

'Because I've asked you to.'

'You don't trust my judgement? I've been a doctor for many years. I know what I'm doing.'

'But I've never worked with you before, and though I'm sure you have a stellar reputation, Dr Bailey, I'd like to make sure that my department is operating at its optimum level.'

So…the sympathetic father persona had disappeared the second he'd clocked on. He was all business, and Brooke had felt slighted that she wasn't being trusted to treat a patient by herself, but would have to check in with Matt.

'Fine— Major.'

She escorted her first patient through to a vacant cubicle and got him to sit down whilst she pulled out a new file. 'So, do you want to tell me what happened?'

'Nothing happened. That's why I can't understand why my wrist hurts so much!'

Brooke frowned. 'Why don't you start at the beginning? When did the pain start?'

'I went to bed last night and my wrist was fine, but in the night I got woken suddenly by this intense pain in it—like lightning, it was. I sat up immediately and rubbed at it, and took some painkillers, but it was ages before I could get back to sleep. When I woke up it still hurt, and I noticed this bruising to the side of it.'

Brooke peered at his wrist. There was some bruising to it—like a dark cloud. Not much, though. 'Have you had a fall recently?'

'Not really. I was crouched down loading the washing machine the other day and I lost my balance slightly, put out my hands to stop myself from falling, but that's all. It wasn't a *fall*, as such.'

She examined his wrist and checked his range of motion. He could bend it and move it around without causing any extra pain. But he said he felt a constant burning sensation in the centre. She touched his fingers, asked if he could feel the sensation, if he had any numbness or tingling. He reported some tingling in his ring and little fingers. Capillary refill was good, and there didn't seem to be any occlusion of the blood vessels.

'I think, Mr Goodman, that you may have carpal tunnel syndrome. The pain waking you in the night is a classic symptom. But I'm going to send you for an X-ray just in case you've got a small fracture in one of the wrist bones, because carpal tunnel wouldn't cause this bruising.'

'Oh, right. Okay…'

'Do you need any more painkillers whilst you wait?'

'No, I can cope.'

She scribbled her findings onto his notes and then filled out a small slip of paper. 'Right, would you like to come with me?'

Brooke walked him to the main corridor and pointed out a red line on the floor.

'Follow that. It'll take you to a new waiting area in Radiology. Hand in the form, they'll take an X-ray or two, and then come back to the main waiting room. I'll call you in when we've got the result.'

'Thank you, Doctor.' Mr Goodman headed off.

Brooke headed over to the doctors' station to transfer her notes to the computer. Her friend Kelly was there too.

'Welcome back! Finally got here, then?'

'Yeah… Hey, why didn't you tell me that our new boss was Jen's husband?'

Kelly smiled. 'Because I knew how guilty you felt about not calling in on him, and I thought that if you knew he was going to be your boss then you would just fret for weeks about starting work and today was going to be hard enough for you! How is Morgan? Did she settle into the crèche okay?'

'She screamed her head off, which caused me to get upset, and that allowed our kind new Major to take great pleasure in letting me know I'd sprung a leak.' She patted her chest and raised an eyebrow at her friend.

Kelly laughed. 'Pads are in now, though, right?'

Brooke smiled. 'Pads are most definitely in. They might be the most unsexy thing a woman ever has to wear, but they don't half make your boobs look good.'

She pushed out her chest to emphasise their impressive size to her friend, unaware that at that moment Matt had come up right behind her.

He cleared his throat and Brooke instantly hunched over and spun in her chair to smile at him, cheeks flaming. 'Hi.'

There was a ghost of a smile on his face. 'How's everything going, Dr Bailey?'

'Erm...yeah...good, I think.'

She could hear Kelly sniggering behind her and made a mental note to kick her under the table later. How many more times would she get to embarrass herself in front of him? So far she'd cried, leaked milk everywhere, worn poo-stained clothes and thrust her breasts out on show like an amateur glamour model. What must he think of her?

'How are things with you?' she asked awkwardly, trying to fill the silence.

He smiled, and she briefly wondered why he didn't do that more often. It transformed his face completely. He was a good-looking guy, but holding that stern, stoic I-am-not-amused pose did nothing for him. But *smiling*? *Genuinely* smiling? He could compete with the best of those heartthrobs stuck on Jen's locker.

'I'm good, thank you.'

'That's great.' She smiled back, wondering what to say, what to do.

Why was this so awkward? She didn't normally have difficulty getting on with colleagues or superiors. Why was talking to him so different?

In her scrubs pocket, her phone trilled. Not wanting to check her phone with him standing there, she continued to grin at him, waiting for him to say or do something.

'Kelly, I'd like a quick word, if I may, when you're free?'

Kelly nodded. 'I'll be five minutes.'

'I'll be in my office.' And Matt turned on a dime and headed off.

Brooke let out a breath she hadn't been aware she was holding. Then she turned to Kelly. 'Wow. Way to go, Brooke. How come he calls you by your first name but calls *me* Dr Bailey?'

Kelly grinned. 'Probably because of my stellar good looks and beauty and because he wants to get in my pants.'

Brooke gaped. *'What?'*

Her friend laughed. 'I'm kidding! We've been working together for weeks now—he knows me more than you. This is your first day. He's just being polite. He hasn't met you properly over a packet of chocolate biscuits and a good mug of tea in the staff room yet.'

'And he has you?'

In her mind she could still see him striding away. Tall. Straight-backed. Determined. A man on a mission. He didn't seem the type to bond over a chocolate biscuit. Not with normal civilians, anyway. She wondered what he was like with his patients. Warm and fuzzy?

I don't think so.

'Absolutely. You don't know the man until you've shared your deep and darkest secrets over a good brew.'

She sighed. 'He doesn't seem the type to do that. He seems quite standoffish to me. At least on duty, anyway.'

'It's hard for him.'

Brooke looked at her friend sharply. 'It's hard for us all.'

'He's stepped into his wife's shoes. Taken her post. And he *knows* that we all knew her, that we all lost her, and most of all I think he's frightened of *you*.'

'Me? Why?'

'You were her best friend. Everyone here knows how close you two got. And when Jen *did* get a call from him, from the deepest darkest jungle that Costa Rica could offer, and got to tell him about her day...she talked about *you*.'

'She did?'

'Of course she did. Jen loved you very much. She

loved us all, but you the most. And he knows that of all the people in the world, you had a special place in his wife's heart. Apart from him, you were the one who comforted her, who gave her a soft place to fall when he could not. Who looked after her as she carried his child.' Kelly smiled. 'You're different to the rest of us mere mortals. He doesn't know how to be with you yet.'

'He doesn't have to be afraid of me. We both loved her.' All the sweet things Kelly had said had caused a lump to appear in her throat.

'He'll call you, Brooke. When he's ready.'

'He's keeping me at a distance on purpose?'

Kelly nodded, then grinned. 'Perhaps he needs to.'

Brooke gave her friend a questioning look. She was being ridiculous! She was no threat to anyone. Never had been, never would be. Men didn't need to worry about her. They never had. Not her father, not Eric, not anyone.

Major Matt Galloway was the least likely man she would want to get too close to. He was abrupt and controlling and…and…

And she'd sworn never to have another man control her ever again. Not after the way Eric had become. That had been bad.

'Do you need to wear make-up?'

'Why have you put on perfume?'

'I really don't think you should wear that *dress.'*

'Cover up more.'

'Were you flirting with that guy?'

She shuddered just thinking about him.

No. Brooke was never going to get involved with another man again. They were too much trouble. Look at Eric! Look at her father! Every man there had ever been in her life had let her down. Walked away when she needed them the most.

It had made her self-sufficient. Taught her that she could stand on her own two feet. Getting pregnant with Morgan and becoming a single mother had taught her that she could do anything, but most of all it had shown her that she didn't need anyone else.

And most definitely—most importantly—she knew that she did not need, or want, the approval or attention of her new boss Major Matt Galloway.

'Well, he has nothing to fear from me. My heart most definitely has a *"Do Not Enter"* sign.'

CHAPTER TWO

'Do you believe in broken hearts, Doc?'

Major Matt Galloway peered at his patient. She was seventy-nine, with fluffy white hair, and sat huddled in her wheelchair, as if life had beaten her down gradually, day after day. Pale, with dark circles under her eyes, she looked as if she needed a damned long sleep.

Yes, he *did* believe you could have a broken heart. Physically, there were lots of ways a heart could fail. But literally...? He saw people give up on life after the death of a loved one—die within days, hours or even minutes of a husband, wife or child. He'd thought it might happen to him once, but his body had stubbornly refused to give up. His logical mind had overpowered his heart and told it to suck it up, because he had a job to do. He had to be a *father*. And his principles had refused to let him leave someone behind who needed him.

'I do,' he said, but he was not keen to discuss his personal feelings with this patient. At work, he liked to remain professional. 'It says here on your chart that you have non-specific chest pain. Your ECG was normal, as was your BP. Why don't you tell me what you're feeling and when it started?'

His patient rubbed at her chest. 'I lost my Alfred three weeks ago. Cancer. After the funeral my chest began to hurt—up here.' She rubbed at a spot just above her sternum. 'It won't go away.'

'And if you had to rate the pain between zero and ten, ten being the worst pain you've ever felt, what would you score it at?'

'A good seven.'

'Does it hurt more when you breathe in? When you take deep breaths?'

'Sometimes. And when I twist in my chair, reach for something, sometimes it can be like someone is stabbing me with a hot pick.'

It sounded skeletal or muscular to Matt. But they'd taken bloods and he wanted to see what they said before he made a diagnosis. 'I'd like to examine you, if I may?'

She smiled at him good-naturedly. 'Normally I wouldn't mind if a good-looking man wanted to see more of me, but would you mind if you got a lady doctor to do it?'

He smiled back, not offended at all. 'I'll just get someone. Give me two minutes.'

He closed the curtain of the cubicle behind him and went looking for a spare doctor. They all looked incredibly busy, hurrying here and there. The only person he could see who was apparently doing nothing, standing by the triage board, checking her mobile phone, was Dr Bailey.

He'd known today was the day. That she would be returning after maternity leave. He'd known that today they would finally get to meet and his stomach had been a jumbled mess in anticipation. He'd heard so much about her—and not just from Jen. Apparently Dr Bailey was a wonderfully warm doctor—kind, caring, well-liked and respected in the department. But Jen had also said that Bailey was the loneliest person she had ever met. It was why she had befriended her. She'd said that this doctor gave so much of herself to others, including her patients, but always seemed somehow to be so alone. Afraid to reach out and depend on others.

He'd not known how to interpret that. Matt had never been alone. Raised in a large family of brothers, he had left them to study medicine, then enlisted. He'd had an army family. A whole platoon! And he'd had Jen, and then the news that there would be a little one coming along.

He'd never been alone until now. Oh, his brothers were always on the phone, and he sometimes heard from old comrades-in-arms, but Jen's death had isolated him. It was as if her death had quarantined him from others. As if he was contagious. There'd been plenty of visitors to bring him food, and to offer to help with Lily, but something was different. He felt tainted. As if people were afraid to get too close to him in case something happened to them too. Or maybe it was a vibe that *he* was giving off, making people feel that they *couldn't* get too close?

Jen had adored Dr Bailey. Loved her. He'd lost count of the amount of times his wife had laughed down the phone saying, 'Oh, you'll never guess what Brooke said today...'

He'd not expected the leaking, poo-stained, crying woman he'd met this morning to be *the* Dr Brooke Bailey. Nor for her to have awoken in him a protective streak when he'd heard her crying at the crèche. He'd empathised with her pain. Remembered how it had felt for *him* to leave Lily with a relative stranger.

The sound of her heartbroken sobs had tugged at his heartstrings and made his gut lurch. And that had been before he'd even known who she actually was! And that brief moment when she'd leaned against him, *into* him, enveloping him in her perfume as he'd guided her out through the crèche door, had made him yearn to wrap his arms around her.

And then he'd remembered she was a *stranger*. Someone he didn't even know. Whom he'd probably never meet again.

Until he'd found out who she was.

Now he would have to work with her, keeping her at a safe distance while knowing that the two of them shared a bond—their love for a woman now gone.

He knew Brooke Bailey had been the most important person in his wife's life—after him and Lily—and he'd been keen to meet this woman whom he'd felt sure would be intelligent, warm and sociable, just like his wife. A *together* person. Someone with whom he could also build a bond. No, he'd definitely not expected the woman he'd met this morning. Emotionally wrought and no doubt sleep-deprived too, if Lily's current behaviour was anything to go by.

'Dr Bailey?'

He saw her guiltily drop her mobile phone back into her scrubs pocket and look up, her cheeks colouring with a most beautiful shade of rose.

'Major! Sorry, I was just checking everything was okay at the crèche.'

He could understand that. The first few days he had left his daughter there he had done the same thing. Lily was the most precious thing in the world to him, and to hand her over to strangers had been difficult. It was easier for him now. He'd been doing it for over a month. Not so Dr Bailey. He had to make allowances.

'And is it?'

She nodded, seeming surprised that he had even asked.

'A patient has requested a female doctor for an examination. Are you free?'

'Yes. I was just looking for you, actually. You wanted me to report in before I discharged my patients.'

He could hear the reluctant tone in her voice but he dismissed it. It wasn't a personal thing he'd done, just because she'd been away from work for a while. He'd asked it of all his staff. He needed to know how the people who were on his team worked.

'Okay. I'll take a look at your findings once we've dealt with Mrs Merchant.'

He led her over to his patient's cubicle and, once inside, explained her symptoms and the results of her tests so far. Then he stepped back. 'I'll step outside.' And closed the curtain behind him, listening as Dr Bailey conducted her examination. He heard her ask to listen to the patient's chest, heard her check the range of movement and finally warning Mrs Merchant that she was about to press on the front of her chest...

'Ow! That hurts!' His patient cried out.

'Here?'

'Yes! Dear Lordy—what do you think is causing *that*?'

Dr Bailey let Mrs Merchant fasten her clothing again and invited Matt back in.

Matt nodded to let her know he'd heard what had happened and to deliver the diagnosis. 'I think you may have costochondritis.'

'What's that when it's at home?'

'It's an inflammation of the cartilage that joins your ribs to your breastbone. It's a very painful condition.'

'I know it is. I can feel it!'

'We'll just check your bloods first, but I think we can safely say we need to get you on some anti-inflammatories. I'll be back in a moment.'

They left Mrs Merchant and headed over to the doctors' station. Dr Bailey handed him her notes from the guy with carpal tunnel syndrome. He'd also got a non-displaced break in his scaphoid, the small bone at the base of his thumb, and she'd given him a splint to wear and prescribed painkillers in case it got worse. Simple enough. Direct, effective, and she hadn't wasted resources on tests that he hadn't needed. Exactly what he'd wanted to see.

'That's excellent. You can discharge him.' He handed back the file, expecting her to walk away from him and get on with her work, but she lingered, as if wanting to ask him something. 'Anything else?'

'Yes…' She looked around her, lowering her voice. 'Jen's locker.'

He straightened, felt his chin lifting. He was defensive because he hadn't got around to sorting it out yet. He'd felt that by doing so he would finally be wiping away the existence of his wife here. Seeing it still there each morning was reassuring. He could almost pretend that she was about to walk in through the door at any moment.

'Yes?'

'If you need someone to help sort it…when you feel ready…I'd like to offer to help.'

Jen's locker.

It was one last tiny island of his wife. Coming back home to the house from Costa Rica had been bad enough. There had been a whole houseful of her possessions to sort through. At first he'd not wanted to get rid of anything, thinking that Lily would want to know all about her mother when she got older. But seeing his wife's clothes draped over radiators and the shower rail in the bathroom had got too much, and he'd conducted a vast cleaning frenzy, taking bags of her stuff to local charity shops but keeping small things like jewellery, the odd knick-knack that Jen had loved, just in case Lily wanted them when she grew up.

Items that were precious—her wedding ring, her engagement ring, a clay pot she'd once tried to make at a pottery class. The pot had gone drastically wrong, and looked as if a four-year-old had tried to make it, but it didn't matter that it was ugly and misshapen. His wife's hands had made it—her fingers had deftly tried to mould the clay—and he'd been unable to throw it out. He knew that one day Lily would hold it in her hands and imagine her mother's fingers in the same places.

There were still photos of Jen at the house. He'd not made a clean sweep and erased her completely. She was still there. Her paint choices on the walls. Her silly magnets on the fridge. Her perfume in the bathroom.

Getting rid of her things had been painful, and when he'd come to work at the London Grace he'd forgotten that she would have a locker here. That was going to be very difficult. Touching the things she'd used and worn every day. Things that were as familiar to her as they would be new to him.

He knew he had to do it. At some point. It had been there too long already and everyone else had been too polite to mention it. Not that Dr Bailey was being impolite. Just concerned. And he understood that. She was right. It was maudlin to think that keeping a dead woman's locker undisturbed somehow kept her alive.

'Yes. I'll…get round to it later today.'

Her mouth dropped open. 'Oh! I didn't mean to force you to do it straight away. I—'

'It's fine. I should have done it a long time ago.'

'I'll help, if you need it.'

'I should be fine doing it myself. Thank you, Dr Bailey.'

He hadn't meant to be so dismissive of her. She was only offering to help him do a task he'd been shirking for too long now. But the tone in his voice had risen because she'd reminded him that he was afraid to tackle it on his own. Worried about what he might find in there. Something uniquely personal, perhaps. Some keepsake that would strike another blow to his heart when it was already so weakened.

She nodded, blushing at his tone, and though he liked the way the soft rosy colour in her cheeks somehow made her eyes sparkle that little bit more, he felt guilty as she walked away with that look of hurt in her eyes.

Had he meant to be so acerbic? Could he not have reined that in? After all, he'd become a master at doing that lately. Putting a tight leash on his emotions. It was easier, after all, to pretend that things didn't hurt. When you were on your own it was easier, anyway.

He briefly wondered who was there for Dr Bailey. Surely she wasn't as alone as his wife had made out? For a start, there had to be a father to her baby. Where was he? Jen had mentioned he was some low-life who had adhered to the adage *Treat them mean, keep them keen.* Though, thank the Lord, Dr Bailey had had enough self-respect to walk away from someone like that!

Matt sucked in a breath. Was he ready to do this? Was he prepared? There could be anything in that locker. Jen had been like a magpie at home, storing away anything that caught her eye, that she thought was cute. He might open the door and have tons of things fall out. She'd never been one for neatly folding stuff and putting it away properly.

Hopefully it wouldn't take too long.

* * *

He didn't know how long he'd been standing there, staring at the locker. It was just a bit of metal. Adorned with all the Hollywood heartthrobs that she'd liked to swoon over and gently tease him about. But it was her name on the door that seemed to be stopping him—*Dr Jennifer Galloway.*

It was like the entry to a forbidden land. A doorway to a world he wasn't ready to face. He kept trying to tell himself that he was being stupid. It was just a locker—it probably just held some clothes, or a pair of shoes and a hairbrush or something, but for some reason his brain and his heart were telling him that this was something he wasn't ready for—getting rid of the last vestiges of his wife at work.

'Can I help?'

He almost jumped at her voice. Turned to see Brooke standing in the doorway, watching him. And, though he'd been abrupt with her the last time they'd spoken, she appeared to be speaking to him with all the gentle patience of a mother to a child. No retribution. No blame. No hurt. Just a genuine desire to help him out.

Matt nodded and beckoned her in. 'I don't know what's stopping me.'

'What stops any of us but the fear of getting hurt?'

He gazed back at the locker. 'I'm a soldier.'

'You're a husband.' She leaned against the lockers and he glanced over at her. 'Being a soldier doesn't stop you from being human. From feeling.'

'I guess both of us have been confronted by things we didn't want to do today.'

She nodded. 'Have you a key?'

He pulled it from his pocket. So small. So insignificant. All he had to do was insert it into the lock.

A heavy sigh escaped him and he closed his eyes, trying to build up the courage to do what had to be done. But
he just couldn't bring himself to do it. What if he opened
her locker and it held her scent? Flowers and a summer's
day? It would hit him like an avalanche, burying him and
smothering him, away from all that was light. He wasn't
ready. But he wanted to do it. Wanted to get it over with.
Maybe if he just…

Fingers enveloped his and he opened his eyes to see Dr
Bailey taking the key and inserting it into the lock. She
turned it, and they both heard the clank of the metal lever.

Blue eyes peered into his soul. 'Open it.'

He didn't want to think about what he'd felt when
her hand had wrapped around his. Didn't want to analyse the fact that his heart had begun to gallop, his pulse
had soared and his mouth had gone as dry as centuries-
old dust.

Instead, he stared at the locker. Hoping. Praying. And
with an unsteady hand he reached forward to pull it open.

A pair of wind-up false teeth was the first thing that
caught his eye and it made him laugh. *Relief!* He picked
it up, turning it in his hands, looking at Dr Bailey in
question.

'She used it sometimes with children.'

She smiled as she took it from him and he could see
plainly on her face that she was reliving a memory. A
memory of his wife that he didn't have.

He reached into the locker and pulled out a change of
clothes—a tie-dye tee shirt and a pair of jeans. Beyond
them were a couple of books that were extremely late
going back to the library, a couple of pens, some soft-
soled flat shoes and a notebook that said *Trust Me, I'm A
Doctor*. And there, at the back, where only she would see

it when she opened her locker for each shift to get ready, a picture of them both on their wedding day.

Gently, he released it from the tape holding it in place and looked at it.

'Your wedding day. How long ago did you get married?'

He glanced at Dr Bailey. 'Five short years ago.'

'You both look very happy.'

'We were.' It hurt to look at the picture, but not as much as it once had. He'd learned to accept it. Absorb it. Grief wasn't something you got over. Like an obstacle. It was something that you accepted, knowing it would stay with you for the rest of your days.

'I wish I'd known her for longer. You're lucky that way.'

He gazed intently at her and nodded, before putting the picture with the rest of the things. 'It's no use either of us living in the past. We've both got difficult futures ahead.'

'Being single parents, you mean? I think it's easier now than it was twenty years ago. At least it's accepted.'

He nodded. 'Who do you have helping you?'

She shook her head. 'No one. Not really.'

'There must be someone. Family?'

'I'm an only child. My mother died when I was very little and my dad... Well, he's never been the reliable sort. We talk on the phone. When he remembers.'

He could tell there was something she wasn't saying. Whatever it was, it was obviously hurtful.

'Any friends?'

'Jen was my friend. The only person who got close. So it's pretty much me and Morgan right now.'

'It's difficult, isn't it? Being alone.'

And then he realised he'd let his guard drop and he stiffened slightly, busying himself with Jen's things, lay-ing them in the box he'd brought from his office, neatly and in order.

He was surprised. He'd thought there'd be more. All this time he'd spent fearing this job, and now that he'd done it he realised there had been nothing to worry about. He let out a breath and then he closed his wife's locker reverently, slid her name tag from the front of it and slowly started to remove her Hollywood heroes.

What to do with *them*? Throw them into the bin?

'I'll take them.'

Dr Bailey closed her hand around his and, surprised again by how her brief touch made him feel, he released the pictures and stared hard at her as she opened her own locker and put them inside. It had been the weirdest thing. Not lightning, not fireworks. More a gentle warmth. And he'd felt...*soothed.* As if a balm had been applied to his soul.

'Thank you. For doing this with me.'

She turned to face him and smiled. 'It was my pleasure.'

No, he thought. *It was mine.*

By the end of the day Matt had already decided that Dr Brooke Bailey was a very good member of his team. She worked at a steady pace, and she didn't order extraneous tests that would upset the department's budget. She got on well with everyone, seemed very popular, and though she might chat a little too much with her patients, rather than discharge them quickly, he didn't think he had too much to complain about.

Before she'd come back he'd heard from everyone that she was a good doctor, but Matt lived by the axiom that he'd make up his own mind about people. He took them as *he* found them, and so far he liked what he'd found in

Dr Bailey. Now the drama of the morning crèche drop-off was long gone he could see the woman and the professional that his wife had become friends with.

As he headed towards the lift, so that he could get his daughter from the crèche, he saw that she was standing waiting for it to arrive, too. They'd spoken on numerous occasions throughout the day since emptying Jen's locker, and already he could sense that a tentative friendship was beginning.

'Enjoy your first day?'

She smiled at him. 'I did! Even though I was fretting about Morgan for most of it, it was nice to use my brain again and interact with adults. I think the most taxing thought I've had over the last few months has been whenever I've had to change a nappy, seen the contents and wondered, *What colour is that?*'

He smiled, having gone through the poo initiation tests that all babies presented to their parents. A sticky black tar to start, which looked like something that ought to be in a horror movie, oozing from a monster, then a khaki green that would hide any soldier in a jungle, and now they were into a kind of peanut butter effect. It had been an interesting journey, and one quite different from the Bristol Stool Chart that all doctors knew so well.

The lift doors pinged open and they both got inside.

'At least I didn't have to examine any grown-up's stools today.'

Matt smiled to himself. Life as an A&E doctor did have that unknown element to it. You never knew what kind of case was going to walk through those doors, from something as simple as a splinter in the finger right through to a dramatic cardiac arrest. That was why he liked it. There was so much variety.

It had been the same in the army. One minute he might

be dealing with a gunshot wound, the next dealing with an ingrowing toenail.

But he liked the adrenaline of working in A&E. The cases that needed to be worked on fast and efficiently, with each member of the team knowing their job, all of them working as a finely tuned machine to save someone's life. There was nothing quite like it.

'All jobs have their perks. Who knows? Perhaps tomorrow you might get your chance?'

She laughed, and the sound did strange things to his insides.

'I hope not!'

He glanced at her briefly, curious as to why this woman, above all others, somehow seemed to make him feel...*what?* Uneasy? No, that was wrong. It wasn't a *bad* feeling as such, it was...an awareness. Like the feeling you might get before a static storm. The air pregnant with expectation, holding a heat to it, a humidity.

Was it because of her connection to Jen? Was it simply because he'd been waiting for her return to work so that he could meet this woman his wife had loved?

That's it. It's because I know she was special to Jen.

He'd wanted to see just what it was about the enigmatic Dr Bailey that had made her so appealing to his wife. He could see that she liked to laugh, liked to enjoy herself and to make close connections with her patients. She liked others to feel listened to and cared for. But there was also a quiet assuredness about her. A silent strength that she didn't seem aware she had. It was her solitude, perhaps, that did that. That shielded her from her own possibilities.

'I'm sorry you caught me using my phone today. I don't normally. Not at work. In fact I don't normally carry my phone with me. But with it being Morgan's first day...'

He waved away her concerns with a swift movement of his hand, staring at the lift display, watching as they ascended to the floor they needed. 'It's fine. We all worry about our children—especially when we're new parents.'

She nodded. 'Thank you. I appreciate that. I really do.'

She was looking up at him, trying to convey her sincerity in her eyes. But it was hard for him to stand there, that close to her, and maintain eye contact, so he looked away. She had very pretty eyes. Bright and friendly. Welcoming. Open. Innocent.

He cleared his throat. 'It's not a problem.'

Was the lift much smaller today? There seemed to be less air. The walls seemed to be pressing them towards each other.

To his relief, the doors pinged open again and he walked behind her towards the crèche, feeling somewhat awkward. He wasn't sure what had caused it, or why thirty seconds in a lift with Dr Bailey had changed things when a whole ten hours with her in the same department had not.

So he walked slightly behind her, allowing her to go first and press the buzzer for the crèche.

Daisy let them in, beaming her ever-present smile at both of them, all white gleaming teeth and bright eyes, showing no signs of fatigue after spending an entire day with thirty-odd children under the age of five.

Matt wasn't sure he'd look as calm and collected as Daisy did if *he'd* spent that long with that many children. He loved kids, he really did, but he was finding it hard looking after even one baby on his own. There was no one to share the workload or the worries with and he missed that.

In the army there'd always been someone to talk to—colleagues, friends and, on the occasions when he had come home, there'd always been Jen. Now his home was conspicuously quiet.

'Lily's been an absolute treasure today! She did a handprint painting for you!'

Daisy unpegged a messy picture that was hanging from a string above their heads, like washing on a line. He looked at it, barely able to ascertain his daughter's handprint in the smudge of red, purple and brown. But her name *'Lily Galloway'* had been written in pencil at the bottom.

'Her first work of art…' He wasn't sure whether to act pleased or show that to him it was just a mash-up of paint on a page.

'Watch out, Michelangelo.'

Dr Bailey smiled at him, mildly amused.

'There's one for you, too, Dr Bailey.' Daisy unpegged another picture, this one in yellow and orange, and passed it over.

They both stood there awkwardly, trying to work out whether the pictures were upside down or not.

'I'll get Lily for you.'

'Thanks.' He collected Lily's buggy from the bay and folded his daughter's painting into the basket underneath.

Daisy came out of the Baby Room, carrying his daughter, who looked as if she'd just woken up, her blonde hair all mussed up and wafting around her head like a furry halo.

'Hello, Lily!' He reached out for her and, as always, was happy to see her reach for him, too. 'Hello, my darling, how are you today?' He kissed her on the cheek, inhaling that sweet baby scent and enjoying the soft squishiness of her little body against his.

Lily laid her head against his chest.

'Wow! She looks just like her mum. She's beautiful.'

He looked at Dr Bailey over his daughter's head, hearing the wistfulness in his colleague's voice. 'Thank you.'

'I mean it. She really does.'

Matt knew she was being sincere, but there was something else there, too. Loss. Grief. It reminded him that he wasn't the only one who had lost someone special. She had too. Her best friend.

As Daisy brought out Dr Bailey's daughter, he was struck by the similarity between the two. Morgan also had a thick head of brown hair that was slightly curling and wispy around her shoulders, and they both had the same eyes. Morgan peered at him, as if uncertain of this tall stranger who stood next to her mother.

He stooped over to put Lily into her buggy and then stood up again. 'Well, I'll see you in the morning. Goodnight, Dr Bailey.'

'Goodnight, Major.'

She smiled back and it so disarmed him, hitting him like a sucker punch to the gut, that he turned quickly and hurried away.

Five months.

It had been only five months since his wife had died. The wife he had loved and adored and had expected to be with right into old age. And yet he was already noticing another woman.

It's just loneliness. That's what it is. Missing someone to talk to, that's all. I don't have to read anything else into it.

He kept his head down as he headed back to his car. Trying to remain focused on his daughter's chubby little legs in white tights, the cute pink trainers his mother had bought for her. He tried to think about what his daughter had done that day, the painting she had done, the way she'd reached for him earlier. He was all Lily had now. She'd never known the love of a mother. Nor would she. He would have to provide everything for her. Be both parents, if he could. Provide the dreams for both of them.

Briefly, he cast his mind back in time to the day he and Jen had discussed moving to New Zealand. How amazing it would be. What a brilliant life it would provide for their future children. Jen had been in the back garden, swinging in the hammock, six months pregnant and eating an ice cream.

'I'd really like to go back there, Matt. My gap year there was the most amazing time in the world. The people were great—really friendly—and there'd be no problem with either of us getting work out there. There's a great little suburb in North Shore City, Auckland, that's perfect for kids. We should do it. Really consider it, I mean.'

At the time, he'd been busy planting some fruit trees in the back garden and Jen had been supervising.

'Move that one to the left a bit. Bit more. Bit more. That's it!'

He'd been home on a week's leave before he'd had to ship out to Costa Rica, and it had been one of the last times he'd seen her alive. He'd only been meant to be out there for ten weeks. He'd thought—they'd *both* thought— he would be home in time for the birth. But after he'd left, Jen had begun having problems with her blood pressure and they'd had to induce her early.

It had still been too late. Jen had had a massive fit from which she hadn't recovered. They'd put her on life support until he could get back from South America and then, holding his baby daughter in his arms, he had watched through a veil of tears as they had switched off the machines.

Just five months ago.

He'd had to adapt quickly, and he'd been thankful he had Lily to look after. His daughter had saved him from falling into a deep depression. She'd anchored him in the present when he'd been in danger of drowning in the past. He'd not had time to dwell on his loss the way he would have if she hadn't been around.

So, instead of never getting out of bed and living in the depths of despair under his duvet, he'd got out of bed. Got dressed. Taken his daughter out in her pram and walked. Sometimes for miles. Strangers had stopped him to admire his daughter, keeping his spirits lifted. They'd had no idea of the tragedy that had recently befallen him. They'd just seen a father out with his child. A beautiful baby girl. They'd wanted to admire her and cup her rosy cheeks and tell him how gorgeous she was, and each comment, each person, had unwittingly given him a reason to keep going.

'You're doing a good job.'

'Lily's okay.'

'She's thriving with just you.'

Jen would not have wanted him to wallow. That wasn't who she had been. She'd been a grab-hold-of-life person. A person who'd squeezed enjoyment into every second— as much as she could. And she'd told him once that when she died she didn't want a funeral full of people in black clothes, sobbing quietly into tissues. She'd wanted a celebration of her life.

Only that celebration had come too soon.

And now he was noticing another woman.

Guilt was a horrible sensation. He'd never really suffered from it before. Not like this. And, logically, he knew he shouldn't really feel guilty. Jen would have been *happy* that he was getting to know her new best friend.

And it wasn't as if he were cheating on his wife. No. He might no longer be married, but he was determined that Dr Bailey was just going to be his friend, the way she had been Jen's.

He stopped for moment and looked down at his wedding band. He hadn't removed it. It had never felt right. Its presence had somehow given him an extra layer of... protection.

But from what?

He decided he would wait to get home and then think about it some more. Right now he had to concentrate on his daughter. She was what was important.

But as he drove them home, as he sat waiting at traffic lights, humming to the music playing on the radio, his mind kept teasing him with glimpses of the beautiful and enigmatic Dr Brooke Bailey.

CHAPTER THREE

OVER THE NEXT week Brooke settled into a nice routine. She only had to work day shifts whilst Morgan was so little, and so each day she would drop her daughter off at the crèche, work ten hours, pick Morgan up, go home, get something to eat and then attempt to shoehorn Morgan into a night-time routine of bath, bottle, story and sleep.

It didn't always work.

Morgan seemed determined not to stick to anything as pre-planned as that. She was her own woman. Already! Sometimes she just wanted her mum to hold her and never put her down. Sometimes she wanted to be rocked. Other times she wanted to lie under her baby gym and bat at her toys, babbling away until the early hours of the morning. None of which helped Brooke get much sleep.

Morgan had no set sleep pattern that she could decipher, which meant that neither did her mother, and Brooke was beginning to notice on her drive into work that she was getting less and less accepting of delays and idiots on the road. Her temper was quick, her fuse almost non-existent. Thankfully at work her love for her job was somehow able to put her bad mood to one side. At least until the commute home again.

Then back at home her love for her daughter and her desire to spend quality time with her, after having left her at the crèche all day, ensured that she forgot about doing things for herself and instead concentrated on just being with Morgan, no matter how it happened. If it meant reading baby board books over and over again—fine. If it meant rocking her daughter in her arms all night—excellent. No problem.

She would do what her daughter needed because she was all Morgan had in this world. Morgan's dad, Eric, was not interested in her—thankfully—and Morgan's grandfather, Brooke's dad, was worse than useless and could not be depended upon. He'd met Morgan only once. In the hospital. He had not seen her since.

Brooke was used to such desertions. It didn't hurt her any more. Or at least she could pretend that it didn't. She just had to hope that when Morgan got older she didn't feel that she'd missed out on a grandfather. Or a dad.

Walking into work today, Brooke was mightily pleased with herself for not having to get changed into scrubs. She could wear her own clothes, having made it through breakfast without getting any baby food on her garments. It was a landmark day! Hopefully, she thought, the first of many.

So she was humming a little tune to herself as she picked up her next chart and headed to the waiting room to call in her next patient.

'Charlie Alcott?'

A young man stood up and made his way over to her.

'Hello, Charlie, I'm Dr Bailey. Follow me and I'll take you through.'

She led the way, still hearing a happy tune in her head, still feeling as if her whole body was smiling. It was good to be back at work and she was in her groove. As much as she adored and loved her daughter, she was happy to claim back her own body and use her brain to help people.

She closed the curtain behind Charlie and asked him to take a seat. 'So, what can I do for you today?'

'I think I've got Addison's disease.'

She frowned. Okay... This sounded more as if it ought to be something a GP dealt with, but who knew? You got all sorts of people coming into A&E, thinking it meant *Anything and Everything* rather than *Accident and Emergency*.

'Why do you think that?'

'I don't handle stress very well and I keep passing out. I looked online and a few websites mentioned Addison's, and as that can sometimes be fatal I thought I ought to come in and be checked immediately.'

Addison's disease was actually quite a rare condition of the adrenal glands that produced cortisol, the stress hormone, and aldosterone. It could affect anyone, but mainly affected women between the ages of thirty and fifty. Charlie was obviously male, and it said on his chart that he'd just turned twenty.

'You say you keep passing out?'

'Yeah. If I stand up too quick I get that head rush thing and dizziness and I have to sit back down again.'

She nodded. 'Okay. Well, first of all I usually advise people not to try and diagnose themselves over the internet. The online world is full of dramatic diseases and bad luck tales, and it doesn't have that real world advantage of examining a patient in person. Because everyone is different, Charlie—you know that, right?'

He nodded.

'Getting that head rush on standing might just mean you have low blood pressure, so let's check that first of all.'

She grabbed the BP cuff that was standard issue in each cubicle and wrapped it around Charlie's arm.

'Right—stay nice and still for me.' She inflated it and took his reading. It seemed normal. So was his heart-rate. 'I'm going to ask you to stand up and I'm going to check your BP and heart-rate again, okay?'

'Okay.'

'And stand.' When he stood, she inflated the cuff and watched him carefully. He grimaced slightly and went a little pale. 'Stay standing for me, if you can, I know it feels weird, but I'm here to catch you—don't worry.'

Charlie stood through it and she noticed on the machine that her patient's BP lowered only slightly, but his heart-rate soared.

She guided him back down into the chair. 'Do you experience any other symptoms?'

He thought for a moment. 'I've always been like this, I think. Sometimes I get palpitations. Like I can feel my heart missing a beat? And sometimes I feel sick and shaky when it happens.'

Brooke nodded, writing down his experiences. She was beginning to suspect something—but it wasn't Addison's and it wasn't something that usually showed in men. However, the one rule she could remember her first ever professor stating at university was: *Keep an open mind. There will always be someone who breaks the mould.*

She'd definitely begun to suspect that this was the situation here, but Charlie would need further tests to prove her theory of PoTS—postural tachycardia syndrome.

It was caused by an abnormal increase in heart-rate whenever the affected person stood up after sitting or lying down, and it mostly showed in Charlie's symptoms. His heart-rate had increased by just over thirty beats when he'd stood up, but that wasn't enough for a diagnosis. He needed an ECG and a tilt table test to confirm it properly. And they couldn't do that here in A&E.

'Okay, Charlie, I'm going to take some bloods from you to check your kidney, liver and thyroid function. And I want to check your blood count, calcium and glucose levels. I'm also going to perform an ECG, which will take a tracing of your heart.'

'There's something wrong with my *heart*?'

'From my initial investigation it seems unlikely, but we need to run some further tests to rule out other conditions. I think you have something called postural tachycardia syndrome, and I'm going to write to your GP and recommend that he refers you for a tilt test, which we can't do here. The ECG and the blood results will be through by then, to help with a diagnosis.'

'Is it dangerous?'

'Well, postural tachycardia syndrome isn't fatal, but sufferers are at risk of hurting themselves by falling or passing out. Whilst you're waiting for your appointment to come through be very careful getting up. Do it gradually, and if you feel faint try to sit or lie down and raise your legs. Drink plenty of fluids, keep active, but pace yourself. Don't overdo it and try to avoid long periods of standing. What do you do for a job?'

'I work in a call centre.'

'Okay—good. Try and stay away from too much caffeine, if you can. I'm going to write to your doctor now and see if we can get this sorted for you.'

'Thanks.'

He looked a little more relieved now that he'd talked over his worries. She was sure that he would be okay, but if he did have PoTS then they would need to rule out any other underlying conditions, such as diabetes or lupus, as soon as possible.

She drew some blood and stuck a small round plaster in the crook of his elbow, and then went to find Matt to report in.

It had niggled at first, when she'd found she had to report in to Matt. Initially she'd thought he was doubting her abilities. But she'd found out that he'd checked everyone's work and approved their tests during the first week he'd started in the department. Apparently she'd missed his starting speech to the staff about wanting to ensure an *'efficient and highly capable department'*, but she could appreciate that.

Now her first week was nearly over and this would be the last day she checked in with him after each case.

I think I'll miss it.

The thought made her feel slightly perturbed.

After her initial annoyance, she'd grown to enjoy discussing her cases with Major Matt Galloway. He was always pleased to see her, always listened intently, and always gave great suggestions for further treatment if she found herself torn between the right way forward. He always told her she was doing a great job and when she'd made a great catch.

Was it the feedback? Was it getting approval? She'd never had that before, from anyone who mattered, and receiving it felt strange. Oddly unsettling, but immensely gratifying. She'd miss not going to him for advice. Miss checking in with him all day long.

He was a nice guy, and she could see why Jen had married him.

She'd struggled at first to match the severe, law-abiding soldier husband to her fun-loving, spontaneous friend. The couple seemed chalk and cheese. But as the days had passed Matt had become more familiar to her, and she to him. His guard had come down somewhat and he'd smiled more, laughed more.

He'd even stood chatting to her one day in the staff room, over a mug of tea and a chocolate biscuit, and it had been just as Kelly had said. He was different when you got to know him and saw past his rules and regulations and the army officer bearing that he used as a shield.

He still wasn't calling her Brooke, though. It was always Dr Bailey and she, in turn, always called him Major. It had become a game. A tennis match. He would serve and she would volley.

She found him labelling a vial of blood and waited for him to finish before presenting her case, running through Charlie's symptoms, her diagnosis and referral.

'I agree, Dr Bailey. I imagine he'll also need an echocardiogram at some point, but we'll leave that to his specialist. That's excellent. I think I can happily sign you off now.'

He looked up at her and smiled and it totally disarmed her.

'Sign me off?'

'You don't need to check in with me any more. I feel totally assured that your practice as a doctor is just the type I need in this department. I trust you completely. You should be happy about that.'

'I am. It's just...' She floundered for words. Her brain had gone blank.

Why was she having such a hard time with this? She'd only been doing it for a week, and she hadn't liked it at the beginning, but that had been before she'd realised just how much she would get out of it. She didn't want to let that go. Realising how needy that made her feel, she frowned, angry at herself.

I am not a needy person!

She had promised herself, when she'd made the decision to carry on with her pregnancy and be a single mother, that she would do so with determination, authority and a belief in herself that she could do anything alone. Wasn't that what she had always done anyway? She was used to standing alone. Surviving without someone else's input. So why should a week of running to Matt have made her feel this way?

Brooke didn't like it. And all of those emotions must be running across her face, because suddenly Matt was standing up and had laid a concerned hand upon her upper arm.

'Are you okay?'

She snapped her head up, determined and bright. 'Of course. Why wouldn't I be?'

He looked at her carefully. As if he were assessing her. As he would a patient.

'I don't know.'

'I know I'm capable. I trust my own practice, I know what I'm doing and even though I've been away for seven months or so it doesn't mean that I lack any confidence in my own abilities!'

She was flustered. She could hear it in her own voice. That and a small note of hysteria. What the *hell* was happening to her? Was it still the effect of all those hormones that she'd had to suffer after she'd had her baby? The bloody things could linger for an age…torturing women with doubts and uncertainties.

You're not being a good enough mother…you don't know what you're doing!

And Matt…? Matt had been drip-feeding lovely words of encouragement into her empty soul and like a dry sponge she had sucked up every droplet of its goodness. Unaware that she had needed it so badly. It was like when she'd been at school, finishing her work before everyone else and taking it up to teacher to be marked and receiving words of praise and a gold star sticker. It had made her beam inside.

Matt frowned and made her sit in his chair. Then he knelt down in front of her, those eyes of his diving into her soul and having a good old rummage around.

Afraid of what he might see if she let him in, she pulled back.

'Go back to your patient. Discharge him.'

He glanced at his wristwatch. He was one of the few people she knew who still wore one.

'It's nearly eleven. We're owed a break. Find me and we'll go for a coffee. In the cafeteria,' he added, which was a special treat, instead of them hunkering down in the staff room.

The cafeteria at the London Grace had an excellent range of refreshments—including home-made cakes that were made on site and were full of calorie-laden deliciousness.

'Oh, I don't think we need to—'

He put his hands on both arms of the swivel chair. 'I insist.'

His voice had softened and that drop in tone went straight to her heart. He was not going to let her get away from this. Perhaps he knew something. That she needed this break?

Brooke stood up abruptly, breaking the prison of his arms, and went to discharge Charlie. She forced herself to focus, giving Charlie the best advice she could to keep himself safe until he got to see a specialist. Then she found herself walking back through the department as if on numb autopilot.

How had things changed so quickly? One moment she'd been humming tunes, sure of herself, and yet sud-

denly she was feeling lost at sea. Cast away on an ocean
with no sign of land.

I'm exhausted!

Tiredness. That had to be it. She'd been so determined
to come back to work and blaze a trail, making sure that
everyone had missed her, needed her back with them.
But Morgan's lack of any need for sleep had caused *her*
to lose too many hours too, and she'd been running on
optimistic adrenaline.

When had she last cooked herself a proper meal?
She'd been going home and just grabbing whatever was
in the fridge—usually a sandwich, or something on toast.
Something quick that she could eat cold if Morgan demanded her attention.

It was impossible to work the way she'd been doing on
hardly any sleep and without enough proper, nutritious
food. Add to that the fact that she was breastfeeding, and
she was totally drained. Seeing Matt throughout the day
had kept her tank topped up. Had allowed her to keep
going from one patient to the next because she'd known
she would get to see him again. She'd become dependent
upon him like…

Brooke swallowed hard and raised her chin. Perhaps
she was like someone that she knew. And the idea of
that sickened her—because she'd thought she was nothing like *him*.

Across the department, Matt caught her eye and beckoned with a tilt of his head. Pulled towards him like a
magnet, she walked over to him and they headed out of
the department to the cafeteria. Matt guided her to a table
and told her to sit down, then went over to the self-service
counter and came back with two cups of strong-smelling
coffee, a bowl of fruit salad and a large apple turnover.

'Thanks.'

'They're both for you.'

'Both?'

'You look like you need it. When did you last eat?'

She searched her brain for any memory of a meal and vaguely remembered grabbing a yoghurt when she'd got home last night. 'A while ago.'

'You're breastfeeding, Dr Bailey. Keep going at this rate and you'll either make yourself unwell or run out of milk. Which would you prefer?'

She felt her cheeks colour at him asking her such a personal question, but then she remembered that first day when she'd leaked milk all over her new blouse. 'Neither.'

'I thought not. You've had that running-on-empty look for a while.'

Embarrassed that she hadn't been giving her all in looking after herself, or as a doctor, realising she really ought to know better, she shook her head. She'd kept herself going on fluids. 'I keep trying to be everything to everyone. My patients. Morgan. I guess I forget about myself sometimes.'

'Sometimes?' He poured milk and put two sugars into her coffee. 'For energy.' He smiled. 'It's hard trying to be both parents—I know how you feel.'

Of course he did. But *he* wasn't the one falling apart in the hospital cafeteria, was he? She pulled the cling film off the top of the fruit salad and forked a strawberry into her mouth. It tasted great, bursting with juice, flavour and sweetness. She hardly had to chew at all, and the next thing she knew she was spearing a piece of melon.

'I bet you make yourself a three-course meal every night, huh, Major?'

He smiled back at her and pinched a piece of kiwi fruit. 'Restaurant standard. I even do *petit fours* with my coffee afterwards.'

She looked at him with raised eyebrows, totally impressed, and then when he started to laugh realised he was joking. She took back the piece of kiwi fruit and popped it into her mouth. 'You don't need it, apparently.'

Matt smiled warmly at her, then glanced down and stirred his own coffee. 'Jen mentioned that you were on your own… You can tell me to mind my own business, but do you want to tell me what happened?'

She broke a piece of pastry off the turnover and ate it before speaking. 'Eric was…' She paused to think of the right expression. 'A learning experience.'

He nodded. 'What did he do for a living?'

'He was an actor—in more ways than one. We met at an after-show party. He'd just finished a run at the theatre, playing the part of the Bard, and I'd won VIP tickets to go backstage and meet the cast and crew. Theatre isn't really my thing—not unless it's got scalpels in it and an anaesthetist—but I went anyway and I met Eric. He was charming, handsome…a bit insecure but he hid it well. At first.'

'What happened?'

'He asked me out, I said yes, and we started dating. I thought he was great. Really nice, listened well, asked a lot of questions, seemed interested in me… But really he was gathering information…to make the best attack possible.'

Matt's brows furrowed. 'How do you mean?'

'It was nothing physical. It was mental. He started going out on his own, saying he was with friends when I suspected otherwise. And because I had no proof he made me feel like a crazy woman for even considering it. But then the comments started—questions that made me second-guess myself. Was I really going to wear that dress when it didn't suit me? Was I really not going to take any of the blame for the fact that he'd lost out on an audition? Was I really going to go out with friends from work when I should be spending time with him? He slowly and methodically tried to close me off from everyone I knew, and when he realised I wasn't going to put up with it he turned toxic. Getting hold of me at work to call me horrible names—that sort of thing. So I broke it off. Something I should have done earlier, but he'd made me doubt myself for a while—made me think that *I* was the one being unreasonable, that I didn't have the strength to leave him. He was wrong.'

'How did he react to you ending it?'

'Well, let's just say he has an amazing capability with swear words and derogatory terms.'

'I see.' Matt looked down at his coffee and took a small sip.

'He'd tried to make out he was a gentleman, but he couldn't carry off that role. Not full-time, anyway. I was glad to be out of it.'

'And when did you discover you were pregnant?'

'A couple of months afterwards. Usual thing—working so hard I wasn't paying attention to the calendar. It was only when I was educating a young girl about her own cycle that I realised the date and I just *knew*.' She munched on a piece of apple. 'Jen told me to forget him, and took me out on the town to show me that there was still fun in life.'

He smiled at the image. 'I can imagine her doing that.'

'She was great. She lifted my spirits. And when she discovered she was pregnant, too...' She laughed as she recalled it. 'She came over to me, bumped her belly against mine and said, *"The race is on!"*'

Matt carefully sipped at his coffee.

'I told Eric about the baby. He might not have deserved

it, but I thought he still had the right to know. Just because he was an awful boyfriend, it didn't mean he would be an awful father.'

'Is he?'

'A rubbish father? Yes!' She laughed again, wondering why she was laughing about it. Because was it truly funny? That Morgan didn't have a dad?

She'd never wanted the children she had to want for anything. She'd dreamed of having the perfect family. Two parents for her children. Children loved and adored from both sides. Enveloped in love and acceptance no matter what.

The smile died on her face. 'He didn't want to know. Said it was my *"mess"* to clear up. That he was with someone else now—as if I might want him back. I soon put him right on that score.'

'I'm glad you did.'

'I was so scared. About doing it alone. I wasn't sure whether I could continue on with the pregnancy.'

She felt awful about that now. Even admitting it was hard.

'I didn't know if I'd know what to do. I can't remember my own mother, what she was like and so I told myself it wasn't the right time to have a baby. I wasn't in a good situation, being on my own, and I had a demanding job, with long hours away. I didn't think I'd be able to do it—not without family to help. But...' She smiled again, lost in the past. 'I couldn't bear the idea of just ending the pregnancy. Jen convinced me I could do it alone. Told me that she would be there for me and that we'd raise our babies together.'

She tried to ignore the lump in her throat as she spoke. Jen had been unable to keep that promise, and Brooke had been so low when that call had come and she'd realised she would be on her own.

'You really have no family?'

She shook her head, determined not to let herself cry. 'As I said before, I have a father. Not that you'd know it.'

'He's not local?'

'Oh, he's local. He lives in Wandsworth. But he's not *present*. All my life my father has had an issue with alcohol—always looking for his next drink, thinking of nothing and no one else.'

'Addiction is hard.'

'You're telling me.'

She thought of how addicted *she* had become to seeing Matt after each patient. She hadn't been knocking back vodka at every opportunity, but she had become very quickly addicted to that uplifting note in her day. To that brief conversation in which she had been made to feel lifted. Better. Her cares gone away. Strangely soothed... her edges softened.

Just like an addict.

'The last time he saw Morgan she was hours old. Then he went out and got drunk to toast her arrival. Wet the baby's head.'

Matt reached across the table to lay his hand over hers. Then his features changed suddenly and he withdrew it again.

She was surprised, then reassured. The warmth and weight of his hand had been a reassuring presence that she'd needed. Needed. There was that word again. How quickly addiction could establish itself...

But why was she addicted to *him*? This was Jen's husband. He belonged to her dead friend. Was that it? Because he represented that friendship and the affection that she had lost? Was she trying to find it in him? Surely it had nothing to do with his dirty blond hair, his clear blue eyes and stubbled jaw. It couldn't have anything to do with the fact that he oozed masculinity from every pore whilst at the same time being kind, empathetic and respectful?

A gentleman.

Matt was everything Eric wasn't.

He cleared his throat. 'I was working on a patient who'd dislocated his knee when they told me that the General wanted to see me.'

She focused on his voice. The look in his eyes. Faraway and sad.

'I didn't think it was anything to worry about. I popped the knee into place and strapped up the leg before I headed over to his office. He told me to sit down, and the look on his face changed to one of such discomfort I honestly wondered if he was about to ask me to examine him privately.'

The ghost of a smile made its presence felt in the corners of her mouth as she imagined it.

'He told me that there'd been a telephone call from the Maternity Suite at the London Grace, and just for a brief second my heart soared at the thought that I'd become a father. That my wife had gone into labour early and already had Lily. But the General looked so sorry for me that I can remember my heart thudding in my chest as I waited for him to tell me that they were both okay.'

Matt stiffened in the cafeteria chair.

'He said that Lily was in the NICU. That it had been an emergency delivery and that Jen had not recovered from complications surrounding the birth. They'd put her on life support and I was to fly back to England immediately.'

He shook his head, as if he still couldn't believe the memory even now. After all this time.

'My brain couldn't compute that. All I could think of was the guy I'd just strapped up and sent on his way. The fact that I had other patients awaiting my attention, you know? It was as if to protect itself my brain had switched off from what the General had said.'

'It happens.'

'I got on the plane home in a daze. Looking at all of these people around me, busy with their lives—couples, families… And yet there I was, travelling back to switch off a machine that would end my own.'

Brooke saw his eyes darken as he recalled this painful memory, empathising with his grief, having felt the loss of Jen, too. Strange how grief could rip some people asunder but unite others. It was a powerful force. It did strange things. Caused people to behave oddly. Out of character.

'I can't imagine the strength you must have needed to find inside.'

He looked at her. 'None of us know the strengths we have until we're tested.'

He was absolutely right. Brooke felt that she'd spent her life digging deep for unknown lodes of strength.

'And none of us know the battles that others have faced or still face.' He leant forward again. 'There are lots of soldiers who come back home and look whole, but are broken inside.'

'You must know a lot of people like that?'

Matt nodded. 'Unfortunately. But we're here to talk about *you*. I don't want you pushing yourself to exhaustion, Dr Bailey. I value you as a doctor too much to lose you.'

He valued her.

As a *doctor.*

He hadn't said he valued her as a friend.

But she'd take it anyway. It had been a long time since anyone had valued her at all, and he was right. Perhaps she *had* been pushing the envelope a bit too much. If she didn't start looking after herself better then she wouldn't be able to help her patients or Morgan at all.

'Message received loud and clear, Major.'

He stood up and eased his way out from behind the table. 'I'm ordering you to stay here until you've consumed everything on both plates, and then at one o'clock you can meet me for lunch.'

'Lunch?'

'So I can make sure you refuel properly.' Matt smiled at her and gave her a mock salute before he marched away.

Brooke watched him go, a surprised smile on her face. Normally she didn't like men telling her what to do, and after Eric she had been determined never to let it happen again.

But there was something different about Matt. He wasn't overbearing. It hadn't been a demand, the way Eric would have delivered it. He hadn't said it to her as if she were stupid and he were trying to demean her.

He *cared.* Genuinely. About *her* welfare. And she wasn't used to someone doing that for her.

She'd always had to care for herself. Even when she was little…sitting at home, waiting for her dad to come back for hours, starving hungry. And when he had made it back the most he'd been able to manage to make for her had been something out of a can on toast.

With hindsight, it was probably the safest thing for him to have been in charge of. And although she'd yearned every day for him to ask her about her day at school he never had. And although she would get her paintings and her ten-out-of-ten spelling tests out of her bag to show him, her hard work had barely received a glance.

Her dad had physically been there, but it had been as if there was an invisible force field around him that she hadn't been able to penetrate. The fug of alcohol fumes had been a barrier she hadn't been able to break through. He hadn't connected to her at all.

She knew he'd turned to alcohol to get through the death of his wife—her mother. But by doing so he had caused Brooke to lose her father too. She'd been so young, just five years old, when it happened and all she had left were photographs of what they should have been. A happy, united family staring at the camera lens.

Coping on her own had become something so natural to her it was always a surprise when someone else looked out for her, no matter how small the occasion was.

Brooke sat there and ate the rest of her fruit salad and pastry, washing them down with the coffee and looking around at the other people in the cafeteria. Families. Mothers *and* fathers. Little toddlers being asked to sit still, to eat up, not to play with their food.

She smiled. It was all so normal for them.

Why had *she* not achieved that? Where had she gone wrong? Eric had been a mistake, but not Morgan. She adored her daughter, and would not be without her, but it didn't stop Brooke from feeling alone.

Had *she* caused it? Losing Jen just after the birth of her own daughter had made Brooke hibernate in the house. Not going out much…not being with people. Not letting anyone in. It had been easier to retreat into herself because that was familiar country. She knew the landscape. There were no surprises if she relied on just herself.

But wasn't life about overcoming obstacles? Facing

the challenges set before you? Fighting to be with those who would love you?

I need to let people in. Open up the borders.

Before I'm deserted altogether.

CHAPTER FOUR

MATT WAS STILL busy with a patient when Brooke had finished, ready for lunch. She sat at the doctors' desk and watched him carefully as he taught a young girl to use a pair of crutches. The girl, no more than eight years old, had a plaster cast around her foot and appeared to be struggling with her co-ordination. Matt kept adjusting the height of the crutches and knelt on the floor in front of his patient, smiling, encouraging her to move forward.

'Standing on your good leg, bring both crutches forward. That's it. Then swing your body forward, landing on your good leg. Excellent! Well done!'

She watched him stand and shake hands with the girl's father, and then he stooped one last time to say something to the little girl, who smiled shyly and nodded her head.

A warm smile appeared on Brooke's face as she watched, and she was still smiling when Matt came over to the desk to finish writing his notes.

'She looked sweet.'

Matt nodded, watching the father and daughter head out of the department, the little girl steady and determined on her new walking aids. 'She fell off a trampoline.'

Brooke raised an eyebrow. 'We ought to ban those

things. I'm sure we could cut down a good quarter of our workload if we did.'

'I agree.' He glanced at her and grinned. 'Though I'm sure our own daughters will want to spend time on trampolines at some point.'

'Yes, well, not if I can help it. I'll be keeping Morgan well away from anything like that.'

'Me too. But we can't wrap them in cotton wool. I know Jen would have *loved* the idea of Lily on a trampoline. And secondary schools often have trampolining in a physical education class. Are you going to ask for her to be withdrawn from those?'

She nodded firmly. 'Yes.'

'And what if all her friends start asking her why? What if she starts to feel embarrassed for being left out? You'll still be okay with that?'

She shifted in her chair. 'Yes.'

'Dr Bailey…I don't believe a single word.' He turned to face her, looking as if he was daring her to say otherwise.

'We all have to do things that sometimes go against the grain. I'm sure I can find other activities to occupy her and make up for the fact that I'm not risking her neck or her back or her ankles.'

'And what do *you* do that goes against the grain?'

She stopped to think. Unsure. 'How do you mean?'

'What do you do with Morgan that's different to anyone else?'

She opened her mouth as she struggled to find an answer, then closed it again when she realised, sharply that she didn't do *anything* with Morgan apart from feed, clothe and change her. They didn't really go out anywhere, except to the local park. But Morgan was too small to do anything. She hadn't even taken her to the local swimming pool for a splash-around, and Morgan *loved* being in water. Perhaps she wasn't the kind of radical, unique mother she'd thought she was.

'You know, there's something I need to tell you,' he said. He looked awkward. Uncomfortable. Whatever could it be?

'Such as?'

'Jen signed Lily up to this class months in advance, because it was oversubscribed. You know what things are like in London... Apparently it's very popular—great for babies' development...that kind of thing...and she kind of signed you and Morgan up to it, too.' He glanced quickly at her to see the effect of his revelation. 'I wasn't going to go, but...' He sighed. 'Perhaps we both ought to give it a try. Seeing as Jen wanted us to do it.'

She blinked. Remembered some vague conversation months back that she and Jen had had about baby development classes. They'd laughed about it. Chuckling about how silly they sounded, how pretentious. How it was more about the parents wanting to show off and have their offspring with a busier social calendar than they had themselves.

'A class?'

'Music Melody. I'm going to go—and you should too. It starts this Saturday morning at St David's Church Hall.'

Music Melody? A baby development class? In a draughty church hall? With a bunch of yummy mummies she wouldn't know, listening to babies banging away randomly on some clanging tin xylophones? It sounded like her worst nightmare.

'I...er...don't think so.' She laughed, as if it were the most ridiculous suggestion she'd ever heard.

'When did you last go out with Morgan to do something fun?'

'We have plenty of fun at home.'

He smiled. '*You* do, maybe. But what about Morgan? This kind of thing will get us out of our comfort zone and stop us from staying cooped up inside. Come on. I'm sure Morgan would love it.'

'But what about *me*?' she pleaded.

Going to a parent-and-baby group didn't sound like her idea of fun *at all*. She'd never been one for parties, or meeting up with friends outside of school. She never usually went to work bashes—not unless Jen had dragged her there.

Jen.

Jen had booked it for *them*! For *both* of them! She'd promised to be there for her, had said they would do things together. She'd *meant* it. Not knowing that she would never get the chance to fulfil that promise.

But Brooke could.

She sighed as she looked back at him, saw the twinkle of humour in his eyes and felt herself giving in. Perhaps it might be okay… And if it gave her a headache then she could take some painkillers afterwards.

'Fine. But why do you want me to go so badly?'

He let out a big sigh. 'Because I want to honour Jen's promise to you.'

She swallowed. 'Her promise?'

'To not let you do this alone. She told me about that.'

Oh. She felt oddly perturbed that he should want to do that. Honour an obligation made by his wife. He didn't have to. She'd managed all these months alone, and she and Morgan were doing okay. But it was sweet of him. Gentlemanly.

'You don't have to.'

'It's the right thing.'

'But we hardly know each other. I'm still a stranger…'

'As all the other parents will be. But I want to do right by my daughter and expose her to as much fun and joy as I can.'

She grimaced. 'Those places are germ factories. We'll probably all come down with bugs. Is *that* doing right by our children?'

'Building up their immune system! We put them in a crèche all day. It's the same thing.'

She supposed he was right. 'Okay.'

'Good. I've already told them you're coming.'

She stood up, grabbing her bag so they could go and get some lunch. 'How did you know I'd agree?'

He leant against the desk, his tall, lean frame effortlessly sexy. Even more so because he seemed totally unaware of it.

'Because you wouldn't let a good friend go to one of those terrible places alone.' He stepped away again. 'I'll probably be the only guy there. I'll get *the looks*.'

'Looks?'

'You know the ones… *Why has he come and not the mum? Where's his wife? Is he single?* You being there will protect me from all that.'

'You don't strike me as the type to need protection, Major. Don't you know how to kill people with just your thumbs?'

He smiled. 'Yes…but I think that's frowned upon at parent-and-baby groups, Dr Bailey.'

Brooke stared at him as he grabbed his jacket, checked his pocket for his wallet and wondered just what the hell she was letting herself in for…

As the days passed Brooke grew more and more nervous about meeting Matt at the Music Melody class. Sitting with him at work for lunch was one thing—but social-ising with him *outside* of work? What did *that* mean?

He knew it was just friendship, right? He knew it could never go any further than that? Yes, she'd socialised with Jen out of hours—but Jen had been a girl. She and Matt were the opposite sex to each other, and it was a fine line for them to walk.

She was already having difficulties with that smile of his. Not only did it totally transform his face, but every time he sent it her way she found herself wanting more and more of it. She enjoyed making him smile. She adored the camaraderie that was building between them. And he had a wicked sense of humour when he let it out. He made her laugh. Brightened her day.

But was that *all* that was developing? She couldn't allow anything else to occur between them. That way madness lay. Just the thought of it right now was turn-ing her insides into all kinds of jumble. She could even feel her mouth going dry. And to think she'd once com-plained about him keeping his distance by calling her Dr Bailey and not Brooke...

Right now she was *ecstatic* that he was calling her Dr Bailey.

You stay over there, Major—that's right. Imagine I've got a minefield around me.

Brooke looked down at her next chart and frowned. Two patients on one chart? She quickly scanned the notes that the triage nurse had added: *Glued together.*

Smiling at the silliness of some people, she headed to the waiting room. 'Rachel and Jake?'

A young teenage couple stood up, their hands locked together, and following behind them, looking less amused, two sets of parents.

Brooke raised her eyebrows at the teens and sent a look of sympathy towards the parents. 'Follow me.'

She took them to a cubicle and got them to sit on the small bed.

'You've glued yourselves together?'

They raised their clasped hands, looking quite pleased with themselves. 'We had to.'

'You *had* to?'

Rachel turned to look at her father and sneered. '*They* kept trying to split us up. Said Jake wasn't good enough for me—but they're wrong! We love each other and want to be together for ever, so we decided to prove it.'

'By gluing your hands together?'

Rachel nodded. 'That's right.'

'You couldn't just wait until you were old enough to get married?'

One of the parents bristled slightly. 'Don't give them ideas. As if *this* isn't bad enough! I've had to take time off work for this—and they're missing school. All because they're so childish they can't see what they're doing!'

Fair enough. She could understand the parents' point of view. 'Can I have a look at your hands?'

She examined Rachel and Jake's hands. They were stuck tight—glued around their palms and fingers. She'd have to be careful not to damage the skin in removing the glue.

She'd heard of other people coming across this in A&E, but this was a first for her. Rachel and Jake probably thought they were being unique and different, proving their devotion to each other, but all they had done was alienate everyone and give their parents even more reason to try and keep the two of them apart.

'Okay, I'll need to check which solution to use on this. Sit tight for a moment. I'll be back in a few minutes.'

She headed back to the doctors' desk and shared with Kelly the details of the case she'd got.

'Oh, I had a couple do that once.'

'Really? What? Here?'

'No, when I worked up in Birmingham. But they didn't glue their *hands.*'

She raised an eyebrow at her and Brooke grimaced.

'*Eurgh!* People do mad things when they think they're in love.'

'It's certainly an emotion that ought to come with a health warning.'

Brooke mused. 'Do you think anyone would pay attention to it, though?'

'I don't know. It would have to be a really clever TV advert. *'Warning! Falling in love can result in sleepless nights, stomach ache and heart pain. Use with caution."*

Brooke smiled. 'Let's not forget the terrible grief at its end. Look at what Major Galloway has had to go through.'

'Matt? He's survived it. He's in one piece, anyway.'

Was he? Or was he just very good at hiding his wounds? Brooke hadn't known Jen long. Less than a year. But they had become such great friends, so quickly, that she'd given her entire heart to their friendship. When she'd lost Jen it had hurt her terribly. And she still mourned the mother she'd never really known, too. Was she destined to always have a piece missing in her heart?

Was anyone totally whole?

Don't all of us have chipped, broken edges?

'I'm thinking of using warm, soapy water first.'

'On Matt?' Kelly raised an eyebrow. 'Could be interesting…'

Brooke smiled at her friend. 'On the two lovebirds in Cubicle Six.'

'Oh, right… Yeah, lots of soap and warm water. Slowly ease their hands apart—no tugging, no ripping. That should do it.'

Brooke stood up to get herself a basin, but then turned to ask Kelly one last question. 'How would *you* prove that you loved somebody?'

Kelly looked thoughtful for a moment. 'Without making them want to get a restraining order? Erm…I don't actually know. How would *you* do it?'

Brooke shook her head. 'I wouldn't. It's all a bit scary, if you ask me. Besides, I've got Morgan now. I don't need anyone else.'

Kelly returned a look that said *I don't believe you.*

She pondered, whilst she filled a container with warm, soapy water, whether someone like Matt, who had already been broken once by loving someone, would ever feel he could fall in love again. Probably not. He had his hands full, too. Both of them had a strenuous full-time job and both of them were single parents. Did either of them have time to fit in the needs and wants of another person who would control their hearts?

Not me. Definitely not me.

But as she headed back to the cubicle and began soaking the clasped hands of the two teenagers, who were still staring into each other's eyes, she couldn't help but think about Matt and how he managed to lift her spirits every moment she spent time with him…

There'd been a frost that morning. The first one of autumn, which was Brooke's favourite time of year. There was nothing she liked better than chilly weather, as long as it wasn't raining. Having to wrap up in woolly scarves, hats and gloves, her nose going red as she watched her own breath freeze in the air around you… And autumn brought Halloween and Bonfire Night, with hot potatoes wrapped in foil and everyone gazing heavenwards at the inky black sky, awaiting the fireworks show.

November the fifth was just a few short days away, and already she'd spent some of her nights listening to the occasional firework or banger going off in the local neighbourhood.

Last year she'd spent the evening with Eric, and as much as there had been fireworks in the sky there'd also been fireworks as he'd walked her home, arguing that she'd spent her entire evening staring at another man. She hadn't. But Eric had insisted that the man hadn't been able to take his eyes off her and Brooke had been encouraging him. One final nail in the coffin of their relationship.

This year she would go to an organised fireworks show with Morgan and delight in her daughter's pleasure at see-ing fireworks for the first time. But in the meantime she had this Music Melody class to get through…

That morning she'd lain in bed, listening to Morgan babble away in the next room, wanting to stay under the duvet. It was the weekend, and she'd been looking for-ward to her customary lie-in of an extra hour. But the class started early, and she *had* promised she would go, and Matt was right. It would be good for her to get out of the house and it would be good for Morgan to socialise, even though she *did* spend the majority of her week in a crèche.

I do need to do something with my daughter other than drop her off and collect her each day.

And who knew? It might even be fun.

She dressed in some old jeans, threw on a tee shirt, a poncho and a beanie hat, slipped into her boots and got Morgan into her car seat.

'Okay. Now, I'm hoping we're going somewhere that will be melodic and harmonious, but as I'm guessing the majority of the orchestra is going to be under the age of one, I'm not holding out much hope for our ears. So if you could at least pretend to enjoy yourself—that would be great.'

Morgan responded by blowing a bubble with her saliva and smiling.

Brooke kissed her button nose and got into the driving seat. Part of her hoped that she would enjoy herself, but would she really find joy amongst a bunch of babies banging away on drums and tambourines? She'd forearmed herself by putting painkillers into her handbag, just in case the place gave her the mother of all headaches.

The GPS directed her through London to the required church hall, and she parked in its small car park, pulling into a space, noticing that Matt was already there, getting Lily's buggy out of the boot of his own vehicle.

'You made it.'

She got out of her car. 'You doubted me?'

He smiled. 'Not for one moment. Are you ready for this?'

'I've got earplugs, if that's what you mean?'

Matt laughed as he strapped Lily into her buggy.

Brooke scooped Morgan out of her own car seat and decided not to get the buggy out—she would carry her daughter inside.

She hefted her onto her left hip. 'What do you think? Are we about to discover this country's next great virtuoso?'

'You never know.'

Matt led the way into the hall and Brooke could feel nerves building in her stomach. She'd never wanted to come to one of these places. What if the other mothers wanted to talk? What if they asked questions? She'd have to tell them she was a single parent. That Eric had never seen his daughter and didn't care. What did *that* say about her, to have got involved with a man like that? It wasn't good, was it? It was hardly a letter of commendation regarding her assessment skills. Perhaps it would just be best to say she'd used a sperm donor?

But, then again, she was here to stop Matt getting *the looks*. Were they to pretend that they were going out? Were married? She'd noticed he still wore his wedding band. That would make Lily and Morgan twins, wouldn't it?

The church hall was warm and in the centre was a large carpet. Around the edges sat various parents holding their babies on their laps, or letting them crawl around on the floor. Everyone chatted happily, waiting for the class to begin.

Brooke sucked in a breath. *Here goes.* She stepped forward with Matt and they found a spot together on the edge of the circle and let Lily and Morgan say hello to each other in their own cute baby way. Mainly patting each other in the face with their hands.

A young woman wearing a bright yellow tee shirt with the words *Music Melody Maestro* on it clapped her hands together to get everyone's attention.

'Welcome, everyone! It's lovely to see so many of you here, today. My name is Melanie and I'm going to lead our group!'

Like Daisy at the crèche, Melanie appeared to be one of those people with a permanently sunny disposition. Brooke wondered if that was a requirement to work with children. Must always look as if you're having the *best* fun!

She smiled and sat Morgan up against her, holding onto her chubby little hands.

'Now, here at Music Melody classes we want children to grow up loving the language of music! And to do that we're going to start off with simple rhymes and songs that we can all do the actions to, so that our babies learn about rhyme and rhythm and melody. Music can touch the soul and bring happiness to all if we all just take the time to find the right song! So let's start with the simplest: *"Pat-a-cake, Pat-a-cake"*.'

Brooke glanced worriedly at Matt. This wasn't an *instruments* class! This was *singing*! Why hadn't he warned her? Brooke was tone deaf and couldn't carry a note! Singing here, like this, out loud, where other people could *hear* her was not a very good idea at all!

But before she could say anything Melanie launched into the song, and so did everyone else around her.

Brooke opened her mouth and pretended to sing.

Matt seemed to be finding her discomfort terribly amusing. They'd gone from *'Pat-a-Cake, Pat-a-Cake'* to *'Twinkle, Twinkle Little Star'* and had just finished a rousing rendition of *'Old McDonald Had a Farm'*.

But that hadn't been the worst thing. Melanie, the alliterative Music Maestro, had said that each parent would have to suggest an animal, starting the verse off *by themselves*.

Brooke had felt horror creep into her bones, her skin crawling, and wished she could be anywhere but there. And as they'd gone round the circle, getting closer and closer to her, her mind had fixated on a goose, of all things, so she'd started her verse: *'And on that farm there was a goose, e-i-e-i-o. With a honk-honk here and a honk-honk there...'*

Her voice had sounded like a teenage boy's—squeaky one minute, deep the next—and the tune had been mangled beyond all recognition, but she'd got through it without her face melting from the shame, and when she'd glanced at Matt she'd been encouraged by his smile and the way he'd clapped Lily's hands together, as if in small applause.

He'd suggested Old McDonald had a turkey, and after he'd got all the other mothers laughing and singing along with him about gobbling the singing circle finally made it back to Melanie and the torture stopped for them all to get a cup of tea.

Brooke got to her feet thankfully, and headed over to the kitchen to stand in line.

'Enjoying yourself?' Matt caught up with her, his face full of humour and bonhomie.

'I'd rather be doing surgery on myself with a blunt spoon, but apart from that it's a thrill a minute.'

He laughed. 'I thought it was your kind of thing. Great singing, by the way, Dr Bailey. I've not heard notes achieved like that before.'

She pursed her lips. 'And you'll never hear them again! I think it's safe to say that I will never, *ever* come back here.'

'Why not?'

She turned to face him. 'Because this is not a class for babies. This is a class to humiliate parents and make them think that just because there are other adults in the room they're actually getting decent conversation.'

'You're not having a good time?' He tilted his head to one side and looked curiously at her.

'Sorry. I'm being a killjoy about your bright idea. Forget me. Go and talk to all the other mummies. They all seem very keen to try and get your attention.'

'How do you mean?'

She raised an eyebrow. 'You've not noticed? It's flirtation central here! I don't think I've seen more women flicking and playing with their hair whilst ogling the only person in the room whose testes have descended.'

He laughed. 'I hadn't noticed.'

But she could tell that he had. It had been a concern of his before he'd even got here, and he'd asked *her* along to ward off that sort of thing.

The queue moved forward and Brooke passed him a cup of tea, adding sugar to hers and grabbing a biscuit that felt slightly soft because it was so old. But it would do.

Had he really not noticed how all the other women had reacted when he'd walked in? Brooke had instantly seen them eye him, straightening their clothes, and a few less subtle mothers had even got out a compact mirror and checked they looked okay before beaming a smile in his direction.

Okay, perhaps they weren't being so obvious that a *guy* would notice, but she had. And she could see why they would be noticing. Major Galloway was a handsome guy with come-to-bed eyes and a rugged demeanour that oozed the fact that he worked hard and knew how to *use his hands*. Probably other body parts, too. Quite…erm… effectively.

But Brooke was immune to his charms. She felt sure of it. Besides, they were colleagues—that was all. They just happened to have two kids the same age.

Not being able to find a chair, she settled herself down on the carpet and lay Morgan on her back next to Lily.

'Jen would have found this place hilarious,' she said.

She noticed him stiffen at the mention of his wife's name. 'Probably.'

She dunked her biscuit in her tea and quickly pulled it out before it could break off in the drink, popping the whole thing into her mouth. As she munched on it she noticed that he was staring at her with a smile on his face.

'What?' she asked through a mouthful of crumbs.

'Nothing.' He looked away.

'No, go on. What did I do?'

He glanced back at her, finally capitulating. 'Jen used to do that. Eat the whole biscuit in one go, I mean.'

'Oh.' She hadn't realised. 'I'm sorry.'

He shook his head, smiling. 'You don't have to apologise. It's just a biscuit.'

'I just don't want to…'

'What?'

'Remind you. Make you sad.'

'A million things remind me every day. Especially Lily. It's good, though. Because why would I want to forget?'

She nodded slowly. 'Has it got a little easier? Since she passed? I know it's only five months since it happened…'

And now she felt awkward for having asked. For her, Jen was the first big loss that she'd ever had to face, since her mother's death. The grief was still difficult some days, but it was getting easier to bear. Sometimes something would happen at work, or with Morgan, and the first thing she'd think would be, *I must tell Jen.* And then she would realise, with a great thud in her heart and stomach, that Jen wasn't here any more. There was a gaping hole in her life and she didn't know how to fill it.

'I've accepted it. When I got back to England I was numb, and then I got angry. Wanted to rage against the world for taking her. But then I'd hold Lily in my arms and I could see Jen looking out at me, through her eyes, and I just knew that if Jen were there still she'd be telling me to stop being such a macho idiot, get a grip and move on.' He smiled. 'Did she ever say that to you?'

Brooke nodded. 'That I'm a macho idiot? Oh, absolutely.' She allowed a smile to play at her lips. 'She hated people being sad. She was always telling me to snap out of it whenever I was feeling low about my situation.'

'Did that ever work?'

'Sometimes. Every day is different, isn't it? Each dawn a new page on which your story can either have a high or a low.'

He nodded, as if he knew what she was saying exactly. 'Jen would want us both to have highs.'

'Not pharmaceutically!' She laughed, the sound escaping her almost like a cry, sudden and short.

She had to look away. Had to blink a few times to rid herself of the tears that were suddenly threatening. If Jen were here she'd be having a laugh a minute and Brooke knew it. Jen *should* be here. Singing with her baby. But she wasn't. And all because of a cruel twist in fate. Brooke was here instead, with Jen's husband, and suddenly it felt wrong. Very wrong, indeed. This was all just too cosy, too soon.

She put down her tea, scooped up Morgan and stood up. 'I think I need to go.'

Matt got to his feet. 'Go? It's not finished.'

'I just need to—'

He laid a hand on her arm. 'Dr Bailey.' He made her look at him. 'Take a breath. That's it. In for three and out for three. Nice and steady.'

He waited until he saw the panic leave her features.

'She would have wanted you here. With us. With Lily. She's not, but she would have wanted you here. To…' he smiled '…*endure* this. Come on…maybe in part two we can make a request. I think we ought to ask for *"Incy Wincy Spider"*. What do you think?'

She was trying not to be taken in by those eyes of his.

Perfectly blue, thickly lashed with dark hair. 'I hate spiders.' She could imagine him leaping to her rescue to rid her of an eight-legged arachnid.

'Then what would *you* ask for?'

She thought for a second. '*"Jack and Jill went up the hill"?*'

He seemed amused. 'Why that one?'

'Jack breaks his crown. I always liked the idea of fixing him afterwards.'

'And Jill? She came tumbling after.'

'Why not? In my version she breaks a bone or two.'

Matt settled her back on the carpet and handed her the cup of tea. 'We can get through anything together. You and I are strong.'

'You think so? I don't *feel* particularly strong sometimes.'

'Like Jack, it doesn't matter how many times we fall. As long as we always get up again. *Do* you keep getting up again, Dr Bailey?'

'I think I do.'

A smile lifted the corners of his mouth. 'I'm glad.'

Brooke made it through the next thirty minutes of singing. At first she just mouthed along, not feeling any of it, but as Morgan began to smile and squeal at all the actions, jiggling along, she soon got into her rhythm and started singing out loud, not giving one jot that she couldn't hold a note.

Who cared? Were the babies going to criticise her? Hardly. And the other mothers? Well, she was never going to see these people again. She could sound like a gurgling gutter and it wouldn't matter.

She was pleased she had come. And she was pleased to have come with Matt and seen him out of their work environment. He was a completely different person dressed in a long sleeved tee shirt and jeans. So strange, having only ever seen him in scrubs or a shirt and tie.

She was fastening Morgan into her car seat, clipping the buckles together and then closing the car door, when she became aware that Matt was waiting for her. She smiled at him and thanked him for asking her there.

'It was my pleasure.'

'Well, I guess I'll see you next week. Have a good weekend, Major.'

'You too, Dr Bailey.'

'Drive safely.'

'Always.' He began to walk away, but as he did so something inside her made her call out. 'Major Galloway...? There's a fireworks display in a couple of weeks in Hammersmith. It's meant to be really good...I've been looking forward to taking Morgan and I wondered if— you can say no...I won't mind...'

Spend more time with the lovely Matt Galloway? Was that wise? Was she being ridiculous to invite him? To offer to spend more of her free time with him?

How is that ridiculous? You're just being a friend.

'Er...'

'If *I* can get through the singing then it's only fair that you get through a few sparklers.'

She could see he was agonising over it. Had she pushed too hard? Was she reading too much into this friendship that he had promised to honour?

'Okay.'

She nodded. 'Great.'

'I'll see you on Monday, Dr Bailey.'

'Goodbye, Major.' And with a small wave she got into her car and started the engine.

Friendship was a strange thing indeed. It could develop at a lightning pace, go places you'd never imagined and hopefully tie you to someone you would trust your life to.

Whilst Jen had been alive Brooke had never really asked her too much about Matt, and Jen had hardly mentioned him. Acting the single parent to be in solidarity with Brooke's lonesome status? It had never occurred to her to ask more about the man that her best friend had loved.

But now she had the chance to know him.

And she was glad that she did.

CHAPTER FIVE

LILY WAS IN bed fast asleep and Matt was sitting on the couch, holding a cup of coffee and staring at the picture on the mantelpiece.

It was a picture that he and Jen had had taken on his last leave. He in his army uniform, Jen with her back to him, leaning against him as his hands embraced the gentle swell of her pregnant abdomen.

They were both smiling. Both of them imagining the brilliant future before them. His career in the army had been going strong, they'd been about to become parents for the first time and were at the start of their parenthood journey.

It was a trip that he had expected to take with his wife, yet now he was walking alone.

It was hard sometimes to look at that picture. Because how could they have known that everything was about to change for the worse? He hadn't known that that was one of the last times he would ever hold her. Hold them both. The only thing he could hold now was memories. And they were fleeting. Like trying to hold a cloud.

But he *could* hold Lily, and she was the burning image of her mother. Cute blonde hair, twinkling cheeky eyes. And that chuckle of hers… It didn't ever fail to make him laugh, too. It was such pure delight.

Jen would have loved to hear it. To be there for her daughter. Neither of them had suspected that she would succumb to eclampsia. Her pregnancy had been problem-free up to that point. Jen had been an extremely healthy person. She'd run half-marathons for charity every year. Had played in the hospital netball team when she could. The news from his General that Jen had been put on a life support machine had been like a tragic joke. Unbelievable. Surely they'd meant someone else?

Yet it had been horribly true, and each night when Lily was in bed Matt would sit in the heavy silence of the house and be thankful for having got through another day. It was all he requested from life now. Making it from sun-up to sunset. He had no more aspirations than that apart from ensuring that Lily was happy. She was his life now. His number one reason for putting one step in front of another.

It had been difficult in the early days. Caring for a newborn whilst in the grip of grief. People—family, friends—had helped as much as they could. But after a time their own lives, naturally, had pulled them away. And he'd emerged from the dark mire of his pain determined to provide the best life he could for his daughter. Not to flit from one posting to another but to take root, to stay in his new job at London Grace and be the best father he could for his little girl.

Meeting Dr Brooke Bailey had been a surprising bonus. When he'd been accepted by the hospital trust to take on his wife's post he'd known that at some point he would meet the woman who had recently been his wife's confidante. And she was every bit the wonderful person Jen had told him about.

And, though he'd only known her for such a short time—just a few weeks—he did feel as if they had a bond. Their mutual love of Jen, their work, and the fact that they were both single-handedly raising little girls. Since meeting Brooke he'd wondered if she sat in her own home at night, nursing a cup of cocoa, wondering what might have been if fate hadn't designated her to raise a child alone? How her life might be different with some-one in it to help her?

Not that she needed someone. He wasn't implying that she couldn't do it alone. But Matt knew what having someone to love and lean on felt like, and he hoped for her that one day she would find that happiness.

The paramedics had wheeled in a little old lady, swaddled in a blanket, strapped to a chair. Ambling along behind them, struggling to keep pace, was an elderly gent whom Matt presumed was the husband.

Tina, the paramedic, handed over the details. 'This is Patricia Hodgson. She's ninety-one years young and a resident at Castle House. Normally fit and well, Patricia was found this morning by her husband, Arthur, with a droop to the left side of her face and aphasia. A FAST test was positive. BP was ninety over sixty and pulse eighty-four. SATS were normal at ninety-five per cent, but oxygen therapy was given anyway. Patricia was di-agnosed with Alzheimer's two years ago and has a previ-ous history of breast cancer during her seventieth year.'

Matt thanked the paramedics and organised his team, including Brooke, to transfer Patricia from the chair to a bed so the ambulance crew could leave and get to their next job.

Patricia looked tiny and frail upon the bed, and he noticed how gentle Brooke was with her as she covered the old lady's legs with a blanket and spoke gently to her, explaining what she was doing.

Patricia's husband, Arthur, stood off to one side, looking frightened and lost. 'Is she all right?' he asked in a frightened, gravelly voice.

Matt introduced himself to the husband. 'I'm Major Galloway and I'm going to be in charge of your wife's care, Mr Hodgson.'

'Arthur.'

'Arthur. It appears your wife has had a stroke and that the event has damaged the side of your wife's brain that deals with speech. I'm going to get her assessed quickly and then we'll get her off for a scan to see just what type of stroke she's had.'

'I just want her to be all right. She's frightened by strange places.'

Matt understood. For Alzheimer's patients, strange places that they did not know could cause undue stress. It was imperative that they keep everything as calm as they could.

'Perhaps you'd like to come and hold your wife's hand?' Brooke suggested.

'Won't I be getting in the way?'

'Not at all.'

Matt issued instructions to his team and watched as they all busied themselves around Mrs Hodgson, taking readings, assessments, and doing so in such a way that they did not upset their patient any more than she already was. The world was a confusing place for anyone with Alzheimer's, and not being able to communicate properly had to be an added upset. Not being able to find your memories was one thing. Not being able to find the right words for things must be torture.

When she was stable they took her to be scanned, to see if she'd had a bleed or whether there was a thrombus, or clot, that might need dissolving. A thrombolytic drug would do that, though there were dangers associated with its use.

'Is your wife on any medication that we should know about?' asked Brooke.

'Erm… I think she's on a statin, and something else, but she's not very good at taking them regularly. The nurses have a hard time getting her to swallow her medication. It's in this bag here.'

Arthur handed over to Brooke a small white paper bag that had various boxes in it. She passed it to Matt.

There weren't any drugs there to treat the Alzheimer's. There was no cure for the condition, although some drugs had been developed to try and slow down the progression of the disease. Matt noted the drugs that Arthur had brought in and wrote down his team's observations on Patricia's condition. It was all done within ten minutes of her arriving.

'Let's move her to Scanning, please,' Matt instructed.

They all walked together to the scanning room and watched as the images came down on the screens. A clot was noted in one of Patricia's smaller vessels and when they took her back to Majors department Matt discussed with Arthur the pros and cons of the thrombolytic.

'You do what you have to do, Doc.'

'Thank you. As your wife is unable to give me verbal consent, it's important that I get your permission. We'll give her the medication and then observe her closely.'

'And then she'll be able to talk to me again?'

Matt could hear the distress in the husband's voice. 'Hopefully.'

'She's all I've got. Me and her…we're the only ones left. She doesn't always remember me, but when she does she likes to talk. Words are all we have. And music.

Funny how she can remember song lyrics from the nineteen-forties yet not remember me.'

'Alzheimer's is a difficult condition. It chips away at people. From one day to the next you don't know which piece has been taken until suddenly it's not there any more.'

Arthur nodded, his face grim. 'When memories are all she has, it's heartbreaking when she loses them. Not for her, so much. But for me. I need her to still be *with* me, you know?'

Matt did know, and nodded solemnly. He administered the drug that Patricia needed and went to update his notes. When he came back to check on her Arthur was sitting next to her, holding her hand as she dozed.

'Are you married, Doctor?' Arthur asked.

How was he to answer that? Yes? No?

'I was. Once.'

Arthur turned to look at him through rheumy eyes, hidden behind thick glasses. 'Was it happy?'

Now, *that* was easier to answer. 'It was.'

'I've had sixty-three years with my Patty. Sixty-three glorious years. There were moments, I'm sure, when she would've liked to have had me done in, but mostly we got on. She was a wonderful wife.'

'She still is.'

The old man nodded and looked back to his beloved in the bed. 'Yes. She is, but...' He shook his head, rubbing at his brow with his free hand. 'I feel selfish sometimes. And cruel.'

Matt tried to work out what he meant. 'Why cruel?'

'Since she was diagnosed with the Alzheimer's I've had to say goodbye to my wife. For the last two years I've watched her slowly vanish. There were times I wanted to shake her, to tell her it was *me*, her husband, to beg her for a moment when she might recognise me again. Then a few months back there came a day when she was lucid. She knew who she was, where she was, who I was—but the most horrible thing of all was that she knew what was wrong with her. What had happened to her and that soon she would be lost again. I've never seen my wife so terrified, Doctor. She grabbed my hands, begged me to stay with her until the end. Then, when the disease claimed her again, I was grateful. *Grateful!* And now all I want is for it to be over for her. So that it'll be over for me.'

Matt listened intently, understanding the man's pain. 'That's not selfishness. It's self-preservation. It's love. You don't want to see her suffer any more.'

Arthur met his gaze and nodded. 'I don't. I really don't. I've said goodbye so many times, thinking it was the end. Now, with the stroke, I wonder if it really is. Because I'm not sure I'm ready.'

'None of us are ever ready to say goodbye.'

He laid a reassuring hand on Arthur's shoulder and stood for a moment, watching Patricia's breathing. As he watched she opened her eyes a little and looked around the small bay in which she was situated, her gaze eventually falling on her husband.

'Arthur?'

Her husband grasped her hand. 'Oh! Patty!'

'Is it time for bed, yet, Arthur?'

'Oh, yes, my love! Yes, it is.'

Matt left them to have a moment alone and went to complete his notes. He sat at the desk, deep in thought.

Arthur had been saying goodbye for two years and it still wasn't enough time. And even though his situation was stressful Matt still felt that the man was lucky. He'd got to say goodbye. To hold his wife's hand. And no doubt when the time eventually came he would have the chance to be with her at the end.

Was he envious of Arthur?

As he considered this Brooke came into Majors with the results of Patty's blood tests.

'How is she?'

'Talking.'

'That's good. That's progress.'

'Yeah…'

He could feel her looking at him.

'Why so blue?'

'Because he gets to be with his wife as she nears the end. I never got that, and sometimes it just makes me feel like…'

'Like what?'

He laughed. 'Do you know what my wife's last words were?'

Brooke shook her head. 'I don't.'

'She was with her mum. Her mum had driven Jen to the hospital because of how unwell she was feeling. She was trying to be bright and optimistic, as she always was, and apparently the last conversation they had was about whether Jen should get her nose pierced.'

He looked at Brooke to see her reaction.

She smiled. 'That's good.'

'Good?'

'Yeah. Because she was talking about normal stuff. Everyday stuff. She didn't spend her last few minutes of consciousness terrified and crying. She was being herself. So…that's good.'

He looked back at the old couple, clutching each other's hands and staring into each other's eyes. 'I never thought about it like that before.'

Brooke glanced over at Arthur and Patty too. 'They seem very dedicated to each other.'

'He said they've been together for sixty-three years. I can't even imagine what that might feel like.'

'Sixty-three years of marriage?' Brooke sighed, supporting her chin on the back of her hand as she leant against the desk. 'I think that would be comfortable. Warm and snug, like a nest. All those years, all that *history*, surrounding you both like a safety net.'

'You're a romantic, Dr Bailey!'

She smiled at him, before her gaze returned to the couple in front of them. 'And a dreamer. But don't we all hope and dream for happiness in some way?'

Matt didn't answer. He stared at her profile—at the way her nose turned up slightly at the end, the fullness of her smiling lips, the gentle way one brown tress of her hair had escaped its messy bun and rested upon her shoulder. It looked soft and silky, and it seemed wrong to him that someone as sweet and lovely as her should be alone when clearly she had so much love to give.

He concentrated for a moment on his notes. *Blood pressure. Respirations. Pulse. Patient.* But his mind wouldn't stay focused. It was as if there was a small cyclone of thoughts whizzing around in there, picking up the leaves of his thoughts and tossing them into the mix—Jen, Brooke, Jen, Brooke.

Lily.

Yes. His daughter had to be his priority. Worrying about Brooke's love-life was not his responsibility. Nothing to do with him. She was his friend, but that was all she would ever be. He couldn't allow himself to think any more of her than that.

But if that was the case then why was the thought of her the only thing he could concentrate on?

* * *

Patricia recovered well, and after a few days spent in the hospital was returned to Castle House residential care, with Arthur still at her side.

Matt had watched them go, envious and yet also happy for Arthur and his wife. They still had precious days together, despite the Alzheimer's. Patricia was still there. Arthur could hear her voice. See her. Touch her.

It was a gift. And having met the two of them was giving him a new outlook on life. Yes, he still missed Jen. He always would—no doubt about it. But he had to be thankful for the short time they'd had together, and more than anything he had to be thankful for Lily and his friends and colleagues.

They were still here. They were here to talk to and spend time with. There was no point in locking himself away just because he felt alone. He had a duty to enjoy life. He'd promised Jen that he would. He'd promised to honour Jen's wish to help Brooke and Morgan. He was *still living.*

His wife, who had embraced life and fun and happiness, would not have wanted to think of him pining away for her. She would have wanted him to be out and about, showing their daughter the wonders of the world. Proving to her that the world was a beautiful place and that she was loved and cherished. Lily was the centre of his universe and he owed her that.

So he tried not to feel guilty each time he smiled, or laughed, or forgot about his grief. He tried not to dwell on it. Sometimes that was difficult. Especially late at night when he was alone and it would make him feel bad.

Keeping busy helped. When Lily was in bed, he'd start on his DIY projects. He'd finally got around to fixing that wonky kitchen cupboard, finally shaved a few millimetres off the bottom of the lounge door, replaced the broken tiles in the bathroom and repainted the main bedroom. He'd taught himself how to cook some recipes he'd never tried before, and given himself permission to relax and read all those books he'd never got around to.

At work he was trying to be more available for those people around him. He sat with them in the staffroom more, rather than returning to his office alone, he joined in with staff sweepstakes and signed up to do quiz nights and charity runs. He knew that everyone had noticed the change in him and it had made him smile inside.

After much thought, he'd finally removed his wedding ring. It now sat on his bedside table, where he could look at it each night and remember the day it had first been put on his finger.

And yet throughout it all he still sometimes felt a little lonely. Despite being surrounded by smiling faces, by people who knew him and cared for him. He still felt alone.

Brooke in particular, kept asking him if he was all right.

'I'm fine.'

'Really?'

'Absolutely.'

'Because usually when *I* say *I'm fine*, it means something else. Like, *Please leave me alone. I'm pretending to be okay.*'

He smiled at her. 'I really am okay. I'm…embracing all that life has to offer.'

'Are you?' She looked at him, assessing him, and he grew hot under her gaze.

'Yes.'

'You're still coming to the fireworks night this weekend?'

A pause. Then, 'Yes.'

'You don't sound that thrilled about it.'

'Dr Bailey, I am most definitely looking forward to coming with you and the lovely Morgan to the fireworks display. Lily will love it.'

She narrowed her eyes at him, her eyebrows wiggling, and it made him laugh.

Brooke smiled. 'That's better.'

'What is?'

'You laughing. You look better that way.'

'How do I look when I'm *not* laughing?'

She paused to consider her answer. 'Thoughtful. Brooding…'

He noticed her blush, which she quickly tried to cover up by taking a sip of tea from an oversized mug. What else had she been about to say?

It was probably best to spare her blushes and change the subject. 'How's Morgan getting on? Still teething?'

She nodded quickly, grateful for the change of topic. 'Yes, but she's not as grouchy about it now. The teething gel has been helping.'

'Lily got a tooth through just last night. She was so much happier when it was over. I got some sleep, anyway.'

Brooke smiled, but he realised it wasn't one of her usual smiles. It didn't light up her eyes the way it usually did. In fact she still looked a little perturbed by whatever she'd been thinking about when she'd mentioned how he was looking.

Odd…

Was she looking *guilty*? It was kind of reassuring to know he wasn't the only one who succumbed to guilt occasionally. But why would she feel guilty about *him*?

Unless…

Oh…

Eager to make her feel more comfortable, he got up. 'Well, I must get a move on. There are plenty of patients in the waiting room.'

She downed the rest of her tea and stood up, too. Just as eager, it seemed, to get past this little awkward moment as he was. 'Yes. My patient should be back from X-ray by now.'

'Anything interesting?'

'Just a query fracture of a metatarsal. He accidentally kicked a metal post.'

'Right. Okay. Well, I'll see you later, Dr Bailey.'

'Yes.'

She looked at him a little uncertainly and the only thing he could think of to do was give her a brief nod before he walked away. His heart was pounding, though, and his mouth was dry. But now he was away from her he could breathe.

Just what was that all about?

A simple conversation. Completely innocent. And then...*something.*

Determined to ignore it—perhaps he'd imagined something that hadn't actually been there?—he scooped up the next triage file and went to call his patient. Patients were good. Patients were intriguing. You could get lost in their problems as you diagnosed them.

And they'll damn well help stop me obsessing about Brooke!

Brooke stared at the X-ray on her computer screen, absently biting at her thumbnail. Her patient was lucky. There was no fracture anywhere to be seen. The kick had obviously just caused a soft tissue injury and that was responsible for the bruising and swelling. He'd just need rest, painkillers, and to put his foot up when he could.

If only she could diagnose herself as easily.

Something weird had just happened with Matt. Something odd. They'd been talking about whether they really felt fine, and she'd mentioned that he usually looked thoughtful, and brooding. And then...

She grimaced. *Sexy.* She thought he looked *sexy*! And as she'd realised that thought her body had leapt into overdrive. Her heart had begun to pound, she'd blushed like a teenager talking to her crush and her body had begun to tingle in all sorts of places! The kind of places that she hadn't used since giving birth to Morgan. And realising that, becoming aware of all that, had made her feel incredibly...what? Mad? Guilty? *Aroused?*

How could she be aroused by him? He was Jen's husband! He was totally off the market and not available, and quite frankly ought to have *Do Not Touch* signs draped around his neck, but...

Brooke groaned out loud.

'Something wrong?' Kelly peered at her from across the desktop.

Yes. She was wrong. She couldn't feel that way about him. Not *him*! What kind of friend did that make her?

'Everything,' she said.

'Oh, dear. Come on, spill—tell me all the grisly details.'

She looked at Kelly. She was another good friend. Married. Happily. Was Brooke going to end up fancying *her* husband, too?

'I hate myself.'

Kelly laughed. 'Oh, right. It's one of *those* days. I've got chocolate, if you need it. Whatever it is shall pass, don't you worry.'

'You promise?'

'Absolutely. Whatever it is will go away. Just like magic.'

Brooke wasn't too sure if that was true. Because now she'd admitted her thoughts to herself it was as if her mind was scrolling through all her previous interactions with Matt and she could see the subtle flirting that had been going on the whole time. Well, maybe not *flirting,* but she could sense in herself all those moments that she'd really *looked* at him and felt *something.*

So would it pass? Or was it something that had been inside her ever since she and Matt had met in the hospital crèche? Had it been bubbling away inside of her imperceptibly, the pressure slowly rising, until now she'd become aware of the heat?

Because it certainly felt as if she had a furnace inside her right now, and it was making her feel dreadful. Because what about Jen? Her memory? Lily? Morgan? She and Matt were *parents.* They both had their priorities, they both had excellent reasons for staying away from each other, and yet...

I've invited him out. To a fireworks night. I should never have done that! And he doesn't want to go. I can tell that he doesn't. He's just trying to be nice and...

Brooke knew what she had to do. Standing up abruptly, making her chair skid away from her slightly, she turned to Kelly. 'Where's Major Galloway?'

'Minors, I think.'

'Right.'

She went off to find him. Her chin jutting out with determination, her mind set on what she had to do to put this right. To end this nonsense here and now so that she and Matt could go back to being just colleagues.

As she passed the curtained cubicles she could hear his voice talking to a patient about what caused gout, and his dulcet tones, dark and soft, sent shivers down her spine. Good shivers. The kind that—

She opened the curtain slightly and popped her head in. 'Sorry to interrupt you, Major, but might I have a quick word with you when you're finished here?'

He turned to her, smiling. A smile that lit up her heart and confused her all the more.

'Sure.'

'Thanks.'

She closed the curtain and stood there, her eyes closed tightly, as she concentrated on her breathing. This was getting ridiculous. He was just a friend. *Just. A. Friend.*

She set off to see her patient with the damaged foot to give him the good news. He seemed mightily relieved not to have broken anything, but she sent him home with some crutches and instructions to stay off the foot for about a week. As she typed her patient notes into the computer she sensed rather than saw Matt arrive beside her.

'What's up?'

Her fingers froze over the keyboard as she sucked up a rallying breath. 'Bonfire Night.'

'Yes?'

'You don't want to go. I know you don't. So I'm letting you off the hook. You don't have to go with me. I'll be perfectly all right on my own with Morgan.'

He looked at her askance. 'Are you okay?'

She nodded quickly, smiling. 'I'm fine!'

Matt raised an eyebrow. 'Ah, yes—the *I'm fine* response.'

Then he laid a hand on her shoulder—supposedly in a friendly gesture, but to her it was something else. Something that was doing weird and wonderful tricks with her insides.

'I *want* to go with you. It'll be…good for me. Honestly. And I want Lily to enjoy it. Is that okay?'

He's touching me. His hand is just millimetres away from my skin…

She couldn't tear her eyes away from her paperwork. Afraid that if she looked into his eyes right now she'd be at risk of losing any last crumb of self-control she had. There were fireworks going off inside *her*, never mind at any display. Her skin felt as if it was sizzling. *Sizzling!* How had that happened? *Why* was it happening? And how the hell could she get herself out of this predicament?

I'm just going to have to keep my distance. Go with him to the display and make sure I keep a buggy's distance between us at all times. Oh, and not look at him. Because if he smiles at me then I'm done for.

'Okay,' she croaked.

He let go of her and returned to his patient, and she was finally able to breathe once more.

CHAPTER SIX

HE SHOULD NEVER have touched her like that. He'd suspected that maybe she was feeling a little attracted to him and he to her, but then it had gone out of his mind as he'd talked to his patient about uric acid and crystals and—

He'd reached for her to show her that it meant a lot to him that she should ask him to come to the fireworks display. Not just him, but Lily too. And yet the second he'd laid his hand on her he'd realised—too late—just what touching her was doing to him!

He'd let go as quickly as he could. Had turned away so he could gather himself and get his racing heart under control.

Bonfire Night for him wasn't just about sharing an evening with her. About watching a firework display in the sky. He was trying to get over something. To face up to his fears. To expose himself to something that he just knew was going to be difficult.

He didn't want to be afraid any more.

Bonfire Night was harmless. He kept trying to reason with himself. Nothing dangerous in it at all. Harmless rockets and cheap thrills, that was all. A few loud noises. Surely he could cope with that?

But now there was the other danger. Spending time with Brooke. Standing by her side, huddled close to her in the cold night, both of them staring up at the sky. She would be smiling and pointing things out to Morgan and he would be...

Matt sighed. He'd promised Jen's memory that he would show Lily the world. That he would not hide her from it. That they would continue to survive without her. That they would not pine, would not spend their life grieving. That they would join in, partake, engage. That he would be there for Brooke and Morgan the way Jen could not.

But there had to be a line. A line he would not cross no matter how she made him feel.

Lily was his world. He could not confuse her like that. Not that she understood, at this age, that she didn't have a mother.

But *he* did. He knew. And he wasn't looking for a replacement. He never would. It was just going to be Lily and him. And friends. Brooke would be a good friend, but nothing more.

He didn't want to admit that he felt disappointment at the thought. That he even felt a little sad. Brooke made his heart race. Her smile lit up his world and he felt good spending time with her. She made him feel safe and warm. She was easy to be with and he loved the way she laughed. It was infectious.

But it was scary how she made him question himself. His principles. His moral duty to uphold the memory of his wife and be respectful of how recently he'd lost her. Not even a year had passed yet!

Here he was, spending time with a wonderful woman, enjoying her company, feeling his heart racing madly, unable to pull his gaze away from her. And it was making him disturbed and afraid and guilty in equal measures.

Was it wrong? To be this close to her?

Whatever the answer was, it would have to wait. The fireworks display was tonight and he would be meeting Brooke there at six. The show started at six-thirty, which was perfect, because by the time it was over they wouldn't be too late putting the babies down for their bedtimes.

Lily's schedule was very important to him. She didn't have too many certainties in this world, but she did have a bedtime, and set naptimes and set feeds. Imposing a solid structure on her had helped him in those painful early days when he'd still been struggling with the loss of his wife. The hours of the day all checked off in a reassuring routine.

For now he was sitting on the floor with her, watching her play with soft, squishy bricks, babbling away as streams of saliva fell down her chin onto the bib that seemed permanently attached recently.

'We're going to see some fireworks tonight, Lily. Big, pretty lights and things that go bang. You'll like that. Yes, you will. Daddy won't, but you will. And you'll keep me strong, won't you? You always have.'

Lily looked up at him and smiled, a bubble forming at the corner of her mouth as she threw one block down on the floor. It bounced and rolled to him.

He picked it up and rolled it back, causing Lily to squeal with joy.

Such simple things. It didn't take much to make her happy. She was such an easy-going baby. Jen would have been so proud of her, their sweet little girl.

'I think I might put earplugs in—what do you think? Will that help?'

Lily offered him another brick.

'Too big, honey.' He smiled at her and took the brick

and, delighted, tried to clap her hands together, slightly missing.

He envied the easy joy of babies. They didn't seem to need much. They didn't seem to have cares or worries. They didn't know great pain or suffering. It was a pity that they all couldn't live in such simple terms.

He briefly wondered what Brooke was doing now. Was she sitting at home too, waiting for tonight? She was probably excited about it. She loved fireworks. He wished he had her enthusiasm.

It would seem that I am not content with my lot.

That bothered him. The fact that he felt something was missing but couldn't pinpoint it. He was healthy, he had a good job, a secure home, a beautiful baby girl. He should be happy. Satisfied.

But it was loneliness that impaired his wellbeing. He'd never been solitary before. He'd never imagined he would have to be. And yet here he was, counting down the hours until he could be with someone again. Someone who lifted his spirits and made him feel good.

Was that so wrong?

Or was he terrified in case it was right?

Brooke was counting down the hours. She'd been looking forward to this for a long time. Bonfire Night—one of the best nights of the year! It never lasted long, but there was nothing quite like forgetting all your worries and standing in the crisp, chilly evening, watching the amazing show up above.

It was carefree. There weren't many moments in life during which you could be carefree, but the night of November the fifth was one of them. And she had one particular fond memory of that night from childhood, when her dad had actually been sober enough to enjoy it with her.

She'd stood there, aged maybe seven or eight, and as the first fireworks had zoomed up into the sky, to explode in a mass of blue and green sparkles, she'd felt her dad slip his hand into hers and squeeze her fingers through her woollen mitten. Such a simple thing, but coming from a man who had been using alcohol to escape the grief he felt it had been an uplifting moment. Brooke had squeezed back and laid her head against his arm, her face turned up to the sky as she'd revelled in that singular moment in which her dad had seemed to say, *I'm here, sweetheart.*

They'd stood together holding hands for about half an hour, and then, when the display had been over, he'd walked her home, settled her into bed and then gone in search of his next drink. The loneliness of being at home without his wife's voice, his wife's presence, had been too much for him to bear.

She'd lived for those brief moments in which he reached out to her. But more often than not he hadn't. He'd told her once in a drunken rage that she looked too much like her mother and it was painful for him to look at her. That had broken her heart. But what could she do? She couldn't change her face, and though she'd tried dyeing her hair different colours she'd never liked the way she looked as a blonde, or a redhead, and had always reverted back to her long brown hair.

When she'd had Morgan she'd vowed to herself that no matter how much her daughter reminded her of Eric she would never blame her daughter for it. Even if every one of her features matched her father's and looked little to do with her mother she would love her child. She would treasure her always. She would never let her daughter feel that type of rejection from anyone.

But she did hope that her daughter would enjoy fireworks as much as she did. For a child they were magical and special, as long as they weren't afraid of the loud noises. She'd heard that tonight's display was going to be extra-special—the fireworks were going to be set in time to music. How amazing was *that* going to be?

Once again she checked she had everything ready. Warm clothes, tights and ear muffs for Morgan, fleece-lined boots, a thick cardigan and woolly hat, mittens for her. Perfect. She didn't want Morgan getting cold. There would probably be hot drinks available for adults, but not for babies!

And Matt would be coming.

Brooke let out a long, slow breath. She'd tried her hardest to let him off the hook, to tell him he didn't have to come with her, but he'd seemed determined. She liked it that he was sure he wanted to go, because at first she'd thought he wasn't. But now that she was experiencing these weird feelings about him she wasn't sure how she'd cope spending all that time with him. Away from work. Where people were relaxed and uninhibited.

She hoped and prayed she wouldn't do something stupid. Like gaze into his eyes for too long, or accidentally brush his hand, or—worse—*kiss him!* Because, heck, even though the *thought* of kissing Matt did spectacular, exciting things to her insides, she knew in the long run that it would be a mistake.

He was a widower. Still grieving. He was *off-limits.* It ought to be the law of the land that handsome, charming widowers should not be hit on for at least one year after their partner's passing, surely!

And she was going to be spending this special night

with him. Perhaps it wasn't all that special to him, though. Perhaps it was just her? Remembering the night that her father had finally seen her, reliving her childish excitement? Whereas for Matt perhaps it was just another night—a few bangs, a few lights, a waste of money going up in smoke. No doubt pretty, but he'd be happy for it to be over, so they could look forward to the *real* best night of the year—Christmas Eve.

Who knew? What she *did* know was that she couldn't let giddy excitement get the better of her. Carry her away on a frivolous impulse to do something stupid. Because— and she must make no mistake—doing *something stupid* with Matt would be appallingly embarrassing. They would have to work together afterwards, and she highly doubted that Matt would be receptive to her lips touching his.

No.

She would need to concentrate and keep her wits about her.

No forgetting his boundaries.

And no kissing Major Galloway!

The place was heaving with people waiting for the display to start. At first Brooke couldn't see Matt at all. Too many bodies…too many people bundled up in unfamiliar thick coats. She thought maybe he'd had a change of heart. Hadn't come after all. The disappointment that shot through her almost winded her. Until finally—suddenly—she spotted him. It was almost as if the crowd parted just for them.

Their eyes met and she sucked in a breath.

He's here.

The breath allowed her a moment to steady herself, get her heartbeat under control again. Back to its normal

pace—or as near as she could make it. But his proxim-
ity, his singular presence, was having an effect on her.
He looked particularly dark and dangerous in that black
jacket, and his cobalt scarf brought out the sparkling blue
of his eyes. Both his and Lily's cheeks already looked a
little rosy in what was for her the perfect November evening. Crisp. Cold. With the promise of a frost tomorrow
morning. He hadn't shaved either. She'd never seen him
with stubble before and it added a certain delicious note
to his appearance.

'You made it,' she said as he made his way through
the throng towards her, using Lily's buggy like a plough.

Brooke saw various women notice him, just as they
had at that awful Music Melody class, their eyes glint-
ing in the darkness, hoping that he might notice them.

Only he didn't. He kept his gaze upon her, his face
breaking into a smile as he got close. 'Just. I've been
looking all over for you. I even considered putting up
a flare.'

She smiled. 'No need for that.'

'No.'

She bent to say hello to Lily, who was sitting in her
buggy kicking and swinging her feet as she batted hope-
lessly at the string of toys across the front of it. Like Morgan, she was wearing ear muffs. 'Hello, little one. Are
you ready for all the pretty fireworks?'

'Bah-bah… Mmm… Pfft!'

Brooke smiled at her and looked up at Matt.

'I feel the same,' he added.

'Oh, really?' she stood up again and fought the urge
to nudge his arm playfully. What was happening? One
minute with the man and she was already feeling flirty.

Stop it, Brooke.

'How…erm…close do you want to get?' She meant to

the fireworks, but as soon as the words were out of her mouth she cringed.

'Er...not too close. You know—just in case the babies don't like it.'

He seemed apprehensive. Had he picked up on her feelings? Was he already at this minute regretting his decision to come out with her because she was starting to act like some crazy woman?

Because, looking at him right now, she saw he looked as if he wanted to run out of there. His gaze was flitting here, there and everywhere, as if checking for exit strategies. Only occasionally did his gaze fall upon her, as if to reassure her that, yes, of *course* he wanted to be here.

Everything about him—his face, his twitching jaw muscle, his body language—screamed that he wanted out. That this was the last place he wanted to be.

Brooke felt as if she was torturing the man by making him stay. Keen for him not to walk away and leave her standing there like an idiot, though, she sought to reassure him. 'It should start soon. Not long now.'

'That's great.' He stooped to pick Lily up out of her buggy and, thinking that was a good idea, she did the same thing with Morgan. At least holding her child she would have no spare hand to snuggle into his.

Both babies greeted each other by squealing and vaguely waving their arms in some approximation of saying hello, causing both parents to beam.

'I think they recognise each other!'

'I should think so. After all the time they spend together in the crèche. Daisy tells me they're quite the terrible twosome.'

Daisy was right. Brooke had seen them when she'd gone to the crèche to pick up her daughter after a long day. She'd often found Lily and Morgan playing side by side, or squealing with joy in the ball pit together. It was almost as if they were sisters.

'Should we get a drink or anything? Are you thirsty? I think they're selling hot chocolate somewhere.'

Matt shook his head. 'No spare hands for a hot drink. I'll survive, thanks.'

She nodded. He was right. They could hardly hold the girls *and* a steaming hot beverage. That would be a disaster.

All around them couples huddled together, and there was the aroma of hot chocolate, tea, coffee, and from somewhere jacket potatoes with beans was being served. It all reminded Brooke of Bonfire Nights from long ago, when her neighbours had cooked jacket potatoes in tin foil and served polystyrene cups filled with hot mushy peas and vinegar. There was something amazing about those familiar smells under the cloudless night sky.

From somewhere a PA system squealed into life and a man's voice welcomed them to the show. There was a little bit of housekeeping—they were told to stay behind the barrier at all times, given fire escape plans in case something dreadful happened, that kind of thing—and then his voice fell silent and a musical symphony began.

Brooke felt her heart accelerate. This was it! The moment they'd all been waiting for. She turned to look at Matt, to smile at him, and frowned slightly, noticing he looked rather hesitant and apprehensive.

But before she could say anything the fireworks began, screaming up into the night sky and pulling her attention away from Matt.

The colours lit up the night sky—pinks, purples, reds, greens, blues. There was a cacophony of explosions from rockets and sparkling glitter balls, whistling comets scattering light like flowers in bursts that split into smaller blasts—all of it to a background of music, the fireworks and the noise perfectly in time with the beat and rhythm.

Morgan was squealing with joy, clapping her little hands together, and Brooke was over the moon that her daughter loved it as much as she did! Her little face was lit up by the display above her.

'You love it! You *love it!*'

She turned to see if Lily loved it too, and was jolted from her bliss when she saw Matt standing there, frozen like a statue, his eyes tightly closed, his face screwed up as if he was in some sort of agony...

'Major? *Matt?* Are you all right?'

She grabbed at his arm to make him look at her, but he didn't open his eyes. He was muttering something to himself. Over and over. But she couldn't catch it. Couldn't make out what he was saying.

Hesitantly she reached up to lay a hand on his face. Standing close to him, almost face to face, she said loudly, '*Matt!* Open your eyes. Look at me. It's okay. Just look at me.'

She was scared. What was going on? Why did he look so terrified? He was an army doctor! He should be used to this kind of thing. He should—

And then realisation came to the fore and she knew what was wrong.

How could I have been so stupid?

Quickly she turned and put Morgan back into her buggy, strapping her in. She could still see the fireworks, but right now she needed to bring Matt back into the present. Because his mind was elsewhere. Stuck in a terrifying past event. She had to centre him. Ground him in reality.

Concerned for Lily, she raised her voice so he could

hear her. 'Matt? It's Brooke. Give me Lily. Let go of her. I've got her. That's it…'

She took the little girl and placed her in her own buggy. Strapped her in.

Then she turned back to Matt, placing a hand on either side of his face. 'Matt?' She waited a moment, torn with anguish at the look of pain on his face. *'Matt…'*

He opened his eyes, his gaze frantic until he tuned in to her voice and then it settled upon her.

As the fireworks continued above them, the bangs and cracks and whistling sound of gunpowder crackling all around them, people whooping and oohing at the sight, Brooke stood in front of Matt, her hands on his face, and made him look at her.

'Keep your eyes on me. You're okay. I've got you. They're just fireworks. They're not what you think they are. You're safe, Matt. Do you hear me? You're *safe.*'

His frightened gaze settled on her own and fixed upon her. 'I…I hear you. I'm s-s-safe.'

'Put your hands on Lily's buggy. That's it. Now, just listen to my voice and follow me. We're going to move away from here. But slowly! No need for us to rush. We're safe.'

She saw his hands were trembling, but he followed her orders.

Feeling sick, and guilty at what she'd put him through, she led the way out through the crowd, away from the field and onto the pathway, and then the road, over to where she had parked her car and beyond.

There was a small café lighting up the street, still decorated with spider's webs and pumpkins from Halloween a few nights earlier. They went in and settled down at a table.

Brooke ordered a couple of teas from the waitress and

gave Morgan a sippy cup of juice from her bag. Then she sat opposite Matt and took his freezing cold hands in her own and waited. Waited for him to be able to speak.

He looked a little worn out, but not embarrassed, which was good. For there was no shame in what had happened.

When the drinks arrived she added plenty of sugar to his and pushed the cup in front of him. 'Drink,' she ordered.

He reached for the cup and took a small sip, wincing at the sweetness. 'Thanks.'

'Is it okay if I give Lily a rusk?'

He nodded and took another sip before he looked up at her face and grimaced. 'I'm sorry I spoilt your night.'

Brooke shook her head. 'No. You didn't spoil it. It was *my* fault. I should have thought that you might have…I didn't know. I don't know where you were stationed, or what happened, but I should have considered the possibility.'

'The PTSD…it's…mild, actually. I hardly notice it until nights like these.' He glanced out of the window at the display that was still thrilling all the onlookers. 'I should have said something when you asked me to the fireworks, but I thought I could tough it out. For Lily.' He laughed ruefully. 'They're just fireworks, right?'

Post-traumatic stress disorder could be a crippling condition. It was an anxiety disorder brought on by a previous stressful, frightening or distressing event. Someone suffering from the condition would often relive that event through flashbacks brought on by triggers in the present day.

'Do you want to talk about it?'

She couldn't get his face out of her mind. The way he had looked as she had held his face in her hands. The way he had felt frozen, chilled by the night air and paralysed by fear. She didn't ever want to see him go through that again. And *she'd* caused it. By bringing him here.

If there was one thing her father had taught her it was that you avoided pain as much as you could. You evaded it, you did what you had to not to face it. The fact that Matt had chosen to come here anyway, knowing how the fireworks might affect him, made her feel proud of him. This wasn't a man who ran away from things that hurt. He was brave, and she wanted to be there for him because of that.

'I was pinned down by enemy fire in Afghanistan. We'd been ambushed. I was part of a medevac team. We weren't heavily armed—we'd been treating the locals, offering vaccinations and first aid, and then we were asked to relocate to help re-staff a field hospital. Twelve men and women were killed when the first trucks blew. Men and women I knew. Had worked alongside. People who just wanted to help, no matter who they were—English, American, locals. It didn't matter. People were people, you know?'

She nodded, listening.

'I dragged a soldier out of the road. He'd been hit in the leg and was bleeding heavily. He was screaming. We found shelter and we had to sit there. Waiting for hours. All around us there was the sound of gunfire and explosions. It just never stopped. I sat there, shivering in the freezing cold, not knowing whether I would live to see the sun rise. And all that time the shooting never stopped. I could hear bullets hitting the walls next to my head. Could hear people shouting. Yelling. Calling for help. But I was pinned down. I couldn't do anything to help them.'

She reached across the table to lay her hand upon his. 'I'm so sorry.'

'It was combat. It happened. It's just hard for me being outside at night, and then the sounds of all those fireworks going off...I...'

He didn't have to say any more. Didn't have to explain. She understood. Could see why tonight had affected him so. But still he had come to spend time with her. Honouring his wife's promise to her friend to be there for her despite the risk to himself.

That meant a lot to her. More than she could put into words. Because no one had ever been there for her like that. No one had ever put aside their own pain like that to be there for *her*. Not her father. No one.

He pulled his hand out from under hers and took hold of her hand, squeezing her fingers in thanks. 'You called me Matt.'

She blushed, nodded with a smile. 'I did.'

'Thank you.'

Unsure of how to respond, she sipped her own tea. 'I've put you through a lot tonight. I'd hate to think of you going home to your own place and being on your own after all of this. I have a spare bed at mine. And a travel cot that Lily could sleep in. Just so you're not alone tonight. If you want.'

She fully expected him to turn her down, but she really did hate the idea that he would have to go home alone after this. She knew what the nights were like once you'd put the baby to bed. Solitude could hit you like a brick. The house was empty. No sounds save for the ticking of a clock to remind you of your life passing with no one else in it.

Matt might be alone, but he had her as a friend and she wanted him to know that. It was an innocent invitation. One friend to another.

Please don't be alone tonight. I can be there for you like you were for me.

'Oh…that's really kind, but—'

'Please. I'd really like it if you came. Tomorrow is Sunday—neither of us have to work. We could spend the day doing something nice. Replace this memory with a good one. Lily can borrow Morgan's clothes if you don't have enough with you, and I have nappies and bottles and baby food. I even have a spare toothbrush.'

She was smiling, trying to think of all the reasons he might say he couldn't do it. She really wanted to spend this time with him. He'd done so much for her.

'You'd have to turn your underwear inside out, but…' She blushed, laughing. 'Come on—it'll be fun.'

He was smiling back at her. 'You've thought of everything.'

'I'm ambushing you again. But hopefully in a good way.'

Matt nodded. 'Okay. That'll be nice. A sleepover! I haven't done one of those since I was about eight years old.'

Brooke smiled back, pleased that he'd accepted. 'I don't think the concept has changed. You stay up late watching movies and eating popcorn. Or I can provide wine, if you need it.'

'I don't really touch alcohol, but I'll have cocoa if you have any?'

His cuteness broadened the grin on her face. 'Cocoa it is.'

Matt made her happy.

Very happy indeed.

And she was glad that she could make him smile. Especially after tonight. Outside, the fireworks were still raging in the sky, but not for much longer. They would leave when it was all over and the streets were filled with happy families.

For now she was content to sit in the café with him, nursing her tea with him still holding her hand.

It felt good. His touch. And even though earlier she'd been determined to keep her distance from him his contact now made her feel completely different.

They were people. People were tactile. They expressed care and affection through touch, didn't they? A hug to make people feel better. A hand on another to say, *I'm here for you. I care. You matter to me.*

And Major Matt Galloway mattered to her very much indeed.

CHAPTER SEVEN

'So THIS IS home sweet home?' Matt carried Lily into Brooke's house and followed her through to the lounge. He hadn't known what to expect, but now that he was here he could see that it suited her perfectly.

It was just a two-bedroomed flat, in a tall tower of concrete and glass, but inside she had turned it into a perfect little retreat. He'd never had the eye of an interior designer, but he wished that he had. Dr Bailey had clearly known the kind of feeling she had wanted here.

There were comfy sofas covered in scatter cushions with cosy throws draped over the back. A bookcase in the corner was filled with well-thumbed books, and next to it was a lamp draped with a silk scarf, a recliner and a small cherry-red table piled high with more books. There was a small fireplace, filled with candles rather than coal, and protected by a screen so that Morgan couldn't get close. On the walls were soft watercolour paintings of animals, but instead of being portrayed in the normal colours of brown and grey they were pink and blue and rainbow-coloured.

It was a happy room. A cosy room. It oozed warmth and comfort.

'I like what you've done with the place. Love the artwork.'

'Thanks.'

He went over to a painting of a swan, created with brush strokes of green and blue, peering closer at it. Then he turned to look at her in surprise. '*You* painted these?'

'I'm just an amateur, but I like painting.'

'They're brilliant! If ever we run out of patients in A&E you've got another career you can fall back on.'

'Well, as I don't see A&E emptying soon, the art world has a lot to be grateful for.'

She went to put Morgan down, aware that both babies would need to go to bed soon. She opened the storage cupboard by the front door and pulled out the travel cot that she'd been given but never used yet. It would be perfect for Lily to sleep in.

Scrunching up her nose, she undid the straps and worked out how to open it. Thankfully it was easy. and she set it up in no time. 'I'll put this in the spare room. Morgan's cot is in my bedroom, so she shouldn't wake you.'

'I probably need to change Lily. Have you got a place I can do that?'

'There's a changing station in your room, or I've got a mat you can borrow if you don't have one.'

'Thanks. I'll give Lily her last bottle and then get her ready for bed.'

'Same.'

They both busied themselves settling their daughters. Brooke ran a bath, so that the two girls could have a bit of a splash, and once that was done they gave the babies their bottles and settled them to sleep.

Morgan settled quickly, as usual, so Brooke had a bit of a tidy-up whilst she waited for Matt to emerge from what would be his room for the night.

She felt strangely on edge. As if she'd had a shot of

adrenaline. She used it to clean the kitchen, being quite thorough, lifting things to wipe underneath, pulling out the toaster, making sure there were no crumbs left behind, wiping down the fridge handles—that kind of thing. It seemed easier to think about what needed doing than to think about how it would be to sit down with Matt in her *home*.

No man had ever made it back here since she'd left Eric. Even *he* had only seen the place a couple of times, preferring to spend time in his own place and make her come to him.

She liked it that it was her sanctuary. Her book nook. A warm, welcoming space that was just for her and Morgan. Their bolthole from the world.

To have Matt here felt…odd. But good.

Brooke rinsed out the sink and then filled the kettle to make them both a hot drink. Just as the kettle came to the boil Matt joined her in the kitchen.

'Finally! Thought she'd never settle.'

'She's in a strange place. Different bedroom, different bed—she was bound to be a little unsettled.'

He nodded. 'Thanks again for offering to put up with us for the entire weekend.'

She smiled at him. 'Not a problem. Kettle's boiled. Still up for that cocoa?'

'If you're having one.'

'Cocoa it is.'

'Thanks. I know I said it earlier, but this really is a great place you have here.'

She spooned cocoa powder into mugs. 'Thanks. It was important to me to get it right. It's the first space I've owned that's truly mine.'

'You've only lived with your father?'

'If *lived* is the right word for it, then, yeah. *Co-existed* might be more precise.' She added sugar and a splash of milk, then poured in the hot water.

'What was he like? Before, I mean…'

Brooke appreciated him not actually saying *before he became an alcoholic* out loud. She sighed, her back to him as she stirred the drinks. 'He was an artist. A good one.'

'Really? Watercolours like yours?'

'No. Acrylics, mostly.'

'What sort of thing did he paint?'

She turned to hand him his drink. 'I'll show you. Come with me.'

She led him through to the lounge area and settled onto one of the couches. She picked up the tablet that she'd left charging by the side of it. She typed the name Phillip Bailey into a search engine and various artwork soon showed up in the results.

A yellow buttercup sprouting through a solitary crack of cement; a rose growing in the middle of a desert; a vibrant tree with thick green foliage living in a wasteland desolated by war.

'He painted hope.'

'Hope?'

'He wanted to show that even in the darkest places life could grow. That beauty and joy could still be found in places you wouldn't expect.'

'They're amazing. Does he still paint?'

'He hasn't touched his palette since my mother died.'

Matt was silent for a moment, staring at the pictures, enlarging one that showed a flowering water lily in an oil slick. 'He lost his belief system?'

Brooke nodded. 'Yes.'

'When devastation struck him he couldn't see the flowers right before him? He couldn't see the light any more?'

'There wasn't any,' she said.

Matt turned to face her. 'But there was. There was *you.*'

Her? No. Matt was wrong. She'd never been her father's guiding light. His North Star. *Never.*

Her confusion must have shown on her face, because Matt went on.

'I've been where he has. We've both lost our wives and I know how that must have made him feel. Words can't describe it. To lose someone suddenly. Without warning. The one person who brightened your day inexplicably taken away. And suddenly there's this new person. This tiny newborn person who needs you the most, even as your heart is open, bleeding and raw, and you feel you can't dig yourself out of the mire.'

'But *you* did it. You didn't turn to drink.'

'No. But I wanted to turn to *something.* Anything that would take away the pain. In A&E we see all the different ways that people numb themselves. It's the human condition. We're not strong.'

'But you didn't do any of those things.'

'No. I saw Lily. Hours old. Wrinkly and squawky and crying. And I realised that what she needed to take away her pain was me. She'd not been held by her mother, so she needed her father. I was the only one who could help her. So I picked her up and promised her that I would protect her to the end of my days.'

He swallowed.

'I was still lost without my wife, my love. I was still bleeding with the pain of losing her. But Lily was my light. My guide through it all. I would have been nothing without her to keep me here. To keep me sane. Perhaps your father never saw that…that you could have been his rose in the desert.'

Brooke blinked back tears. 'He told me he couldn't look at me. That I reminded him too much of my mother.'

'I see Jen in Lily, too.'

'So why didn't my father hold on to *me*? Why did he not care? Why did he walk away from me when it mattered? If I was his light?'

Matt shook his head. 'I can't answer for him. I don't know.'

'He was weak. You're strong. That's the difference.'

'I'm not strong.'

'Yes, you are. All that you've been through and yet you're here. Lily's father. Dedicated, hard-working. *Sober.* A soldier who went to war and survived. You've got scars, but you've never weakened. Being a father is what drives you and I've never been enough to drive anyone.'

The words were out before she could stop them, and her cheeks coloured.

'Sorry—ignore that. I was just having a pity party. It's over now.' She gave a brief smile and sipped at her cocoa.

'You're entitled to be mad at him. He let you down. But I really don't think there's anything you could say to him that he hasn't already said to himself. He's still in hell, I'd say. The drink puts out some of the flames. For a while. But then when the pain comes back…the regret, the sorrow…'

'He goes back to the booze. To numb himself again.'

Could it be true? That her father hated himself for what he'd done to her? That he berated himself day after day after day for letting all these years pass, letting his baby grow into a woman and still not putting things right?

'Lily's lucky to have you. If my father had been *half* the man you are…' She glanced at him, not intending to hold his gaze, but she did.

The intensity in his eyes was shocking. It was as if he could see deep inside her soul and liked what he saw. As if he saw *her*. Not the public persona—not Dr Bailey, A&E consultant, a single mum—he saw *her*. The frightened, self-doubting version. But even seeing her vulnerable and exposed like that didn't make him turn away.

He was staying. Interested. Intrigued.

It was too much.

Brooke stood up, still holding her mug. 'Well, it's… er…been a long day. I ought to…turn in.' She vaguely waved her arm in the direction of her bedroom. 'Goodnight, Major.'

He stood up, facing her. 'Goodnight, Dr Bailey.'

She had to tear her gaze away. It was hard. As if he was a magnet, pulling her in, and it took every ounce of her nerve and strength to walk in the other direction.

Brooke lay in bed and stared at the ceiling.

Morgan was sleeping soundly in her cot, one little fist tucked up underneath her chin, her other arm cast over her head. She'd be good now, at least. The latest teething episode seemed to be over, which meant Brooke should be getting a full night of sleep.

But sleep remained elusive. Out of arm's reach. Ridiculously, she felt wide awake, and completely physically aware that Matt was just in the next room to hers. Literally feet away. Separated by a wall. A line of bricks. That was it.

He was in the next room!

She'd bet that he was asleep. He'd had a stressful evening, what with the panic attack at the display. The adrenaline of that must have made him tired. He was probably snoozing away in dreamland, completely unaware of where he was. Where *she* was.

Through a small slit in her curtains she could see the stars in the night sky. Twinkling points of light in the darkness.

Could it be true what Matt had said about her father? She'd always been angry with him for not being there for her, at the fact that he never wanted to talk about her mother or even spend any time with his daughter. She'd thought it was because she was worthless. Why else would he ignore her?

It had never occurred to her that it was too painful for him. That he'd loved her mother so much that the pain of her loss was too much. Because human beings didn't deal with pain very well. Self-medicating with whatever worked to take the pain away—pills, drugs, alcohol, cigarettes, food. When a child cried and wouldn't stop what did most parents do? They offered a biscuit or another indulgent treat, teaching children that to make the pain go away you filled yourself with something else instead.

Was her father still trying to make himself feel better? Could that be it? Perhaps it wasn't that *she* was worthless, not worth loving. It was just that he couldn't cope and had found the thing that worked for him, no matter how bad it was. He might once have made a living painting hope, but what if she who *should* have been his hope, his light in the darkness of his grief, had been too bright for him to look at?

Who wouldn't give anything to be numb when pain struck?

Yet Matt had pushed through *his* pain. Had been able to put his pain to one side so he could be there for his baby. He was solid. Dependable.

Attractive, gorgeous, a gentleman...

She let out a heavy breath and turned to her bedside table for her glass of water.

Damn! I didn't bring one in, did I? I was in such a hurry to escape that look in his eyes.

She needed a drink. She felt parched. And now she was aware of it she'd focus on it so much she'd never get any sleep!

Matt was bound to be asleep, right? If she crept out there, past his room, he'd never hear her go into the kitchen for a glass of water. It wasn't as if she was going to put the kettle on, or anything. She would be safe, right?

Perhaps I don't need a drink of water that badly?

Only she really did. And her legs felt restless. She needed to get up and walk, and he was in another room. It wasn't as if he was sleeping on the couch or anything.

Having persuaded herself that it would be safe to go and get her drink, Brooke threw back the covers and swung her legs out of bed. She wrapped her robe around her waist and carefully opened the door, aware that the bedroom door might make a sound at its widest point. She slipped through the gap and padded down the hallway, past his bedroom door and into the kitchen.

She breathed a sigh of relief and switched on the light. Blinking rapidly, she quietly opened the kitchen cupboard and grabbed a glass, filling it with water from the tap. Taking a long swallow of the refreshing fluid, she turned to go—and saw Matt standing in the doorway.

Instantly her heart began to pound. He was wearing only a tee shirt and boxers, and she couldn't help but notice his fine arms and long, muscled legs.

'I hope I didn't scare you—I needed a drink. I usually have one beside my bed, but being in a strange place I forgot all about it,' he explained.

'Same. About needing the drink, that is.' She gestured with her glass and smiled, noticing his hair looked a little ruffled, as if he'd been tossing and turning. 'Lily still asleep?'

'Out like a light.'

'Good.'

It was as if she couldn't take her eyes off him. He filled her vision.

'I'd best be getting back, then.' She went to move past him, through the doorway, and he did step to one side so that she could pass. But she made the mistake of looking up at him and smiling her thanks as she did so. Pausing. Ever so briefly.

His gaze locked with hers and she could read desire in his eyes—apprehension, fear, but most of all yearning.

She wanted to kiss him so badly, but she didn't want to overstep the mark in case he—

Matt stepped forward, his gaze going to her lips, then to her eyes, then her lips again.

Brooke's breathing changed and she stared back, taking in all the features of this beautiful man up close.

They weren't touching. Neither of them was overstepping their boundary, but both were fighting the urge to reach out and take what they wanted.

'Brooke, I…'

She looked directly into his soul. He'd said her name. 'You called me Brooke.'

'Yes.'

'Not Dr Bailey.'

'No.'

And he came ever closer, watching her intently, as if he expected her to place her hand on his chest at any moment to stop him. But she didn't stop him. She wanted him close to her—wanted to see what it would feel like. She wanted him to kiss her.

Brooke closed her eyes as his head dipped and his lips

touched hers—feather-light, brief. She stood there, her entire nervous system lit up like the national grid, waiting, anticipating more.

And he gave her what she wanted.

His hands came up to cradle each side of her face as he drew her to him and deepened the kiss.

Her whole body ached, desiring more of him as she kissed him back. He was all she could think of, and his lips, his kiss, fuelled a fire inside her that had long lain dormant.

All thoughts of caution, of whether this was right or wrong, went straight out of her head. All that seemed to matter to her at that moment was that he continued to kiss her.

Hesitantly, her arms embraced him, feeling the raw, hard muscles beneath his skin.

This man desired her. Wanted her. She had not expected this. She'd known—felt—that she was developing feelings of attraction for him, but she had told herself it was one-sided. That he would not feel the same. And yet here they were...

What did this mean? Was it just one kiss, or would it be more? She wanted more. Wanted to give in to what she was feeling right now and take all of him. Have everything he could offer right now and the future be damned!

But...they had to work together. They had their children to consider. They had to be responsible.

'Matt.' She broke the kiss and, breathing heavily, stared deeply into his eyes. 'We need to think about this.'

He stared back, then nodded, releasing her. And as he did so disappointment entered every cell in her body. She'd felt on fire, and instead of allowing herself to blaze she had doused the flames. She hated herself for doing so.

'You're right.' He stepped back, leaning his body against the doorframe.

She mirrored his movements opposite. 'We're work colleagues…we…' She couldn't think of what else to say. Her body, her mind was screaming at her to forget the doubts, just kiss him again!

'Have to be sensible?' He finished for her.

'Yes.'

No!

They stared at each other for a moment more, and then suddenly they were back in each other's arms, their lips pressed against each other's, the long lengths of their bodies pressed tight as his tongue found hers and she groaned.

She *needed* him. More than she had ever allowed herself to need a man. She didn't care about the consequences now. *Need* trumped everything else, and she cast her hesitations aside as quickly as he cast aside her robe.

She could feel him against her, his desire pressing into her, and then she was reaching for his tee shirt to pull it free over his head.

They staggered into the lounge and Matt reached under her long tee. She felt the wondrous heat of his hands upon her bare flesh, her breasts, and it was *everything*. His touch, his taste, his heat. It fed her. It was life.

How was it possible that he could make her feel this way? It had never felt this *urgent* with Eric and he was the father of her child. It hadn't felt this way *ever*. With any man. Not this intensity. Not this much.

Was it because there was already so much history between them? Even before they'd met they'd shared a history. A love for the same person. And that bond, that strength they shared, had pulled them together.

They were the same, Matt and her. Both traumatised,

both alone, both single parents facing the same struggles in the same work environment. Both of them hurt by previous encounters. There was a saying that misery liked company... Did hurt people naturally seek each other out?

No. It had to be more than that for them. They shared the same wound. They were two halves of the same scar. Perhaps that was why it felt so right to be in his arms. Because only together could they heal.

Brooke breathed his name as he moved into her. Felt the force of his need within her and sighed delightfully. This felt *right*. That was what counted. Even though she had tried to fight it, tried to keep her distance. Perhaps the reason they had failed at that was because they were meant to be?

No. She wouldn't allow herself to think that far ahead. Experience had taught her that people generally let her down. People she had thought she could rely on.

What mattered was the here and now. She would deal with today and not worry about tomorrow.

Not yet.

And it helped that the today—the *now*—felt so damned good!

He woke in Brooke's bed. It was still dark and the sun had not yet risen. He was used to waking early. A habit from his early army days, when he'd tried to cheat the agony of the drill sergeant crashing into his dorm, shouting and yelling.

He still liked to wake early. To lie there for a moment and mentally prepare himself for the day. It was a habit that had come in handy after Jen had died. He'd lie there for a few minutes, thinking of all he had to do to get through the day. Things that Lily would need. Things he would need to get done in the house. Whether they would need to go food shopping. The five-mile walk he would try to fit in, with Lily in her buggy, because it was important to get out of the house and not pine away in grief.

Grief, guilt, sorrow—they were all time-stealers and he could never allow them a place in his life. Not until he had control back. Not until the intensity of that grief had been absorbed and wasn't as sharp as it had been.

It took a moment or two for him to remind himself of where he was. Not his own home...not his own bed.

Brooke's bed. And she was in his arms as he spooned her. He inhaled her scent, her perfume, as she lay there and felt a pang in his heart.

She looked so beautiful. Her long dark hair over the pillow. Her naked shoulders so smooth and feminine. The feel of the length of her against his body.

His own body stirred in response and he closed his eyes to regain control of himself.

Last night had been...*amazing.* A gift that he hadn't expected at all. He'd been lying there, staring at the ceiling, unable to get his pillows right, tossing and turning, berating himself for his forbidden feelings for this woman who wasn't his wife.

His attraction for her had been growing steadily. He'd known that for a long time. But he'd told himself over and over that he would control it and do nothing about it—because it wasn't right.

But at the fireworks display he'd lost the present, had been thrown right back into the horror of Khost Province in Afghanistan. And as he'd heard the cracks and whistles of the fireworks he'd seen in his head the two trucks ahead of him being blown off their axles and thrown to one side. Felt the rush of adrenaline as he'd taken cover, aware that a bullet might rip through his heart at any second, but still going back for a fallen comrade.

He had no longer been standing in a field, watching fireworks with delight, he'd been back there, cowering under a hail of bullets, and she—Brooke—had brought him out of that.

He would not have thought it possible. But her touch, her voice, her insistence that he listen to her, had cut through the hell in his mind and pulled him out of his terror.

Her eyes... That look in her eyes had held him in the present and made him breathe, made him take root in reality again, and he'd been so thankful for that. When she'd said that she didn't want him to be alone he'd been grateful. The idea of returning home with Lily to put her to bed and be alone again with his torturous thoughts had been enough to make him accept.

He'd not said yes to get her into bed. He'd not said yes to see what would happen. He'd said yes because he'd genuinely wanted to be with her. To be wrapped in her protection and soothed by her presence, knowing she was just in the next room. Not to be alone again. Not again. Just for one night.

He'd got up for a drink not knowing that she was already up, and when he'd walked out of his room and seen that the kitchen light was on he'd almost faltered. Had almost gone back to his room. Only he hadn't. He'd wanted to see her. To say goodnight properly.

And then he'd kissed her.

Again, *she* had been the strong one—had tried to make them pause for a moment. Take a breather. Think things through. And he'd tried... But he'd still had the taste of her on his lips and he'd stamped down on all the doubt, on all the voices in his head telling him it was a

bad idea, because his body, his being, had been screaming that it needed her. That she was the other half of himself. The one who could save him.

And like a drowning man grabbing at a buoy, he'd
reached out and pulled her towards him, felt his soul
drowning in the pleasure of her touch, her kiss, her
heat—so much so that all logical thought had gone out
of his head.

But now the cold light of day was approaching. He
could feel it. Inching closer over the horizon accompa-
nied by his old friends guilt and doubt.

*I buried my wife just months ago and already I'm in
another woman's bed.*

Brooke thought he was strong. But he wasn't. He was
weak. And he'd proved that. Sleeping with Brooke, staying the night with her, had been everything he might have
dreamed of—but now he felt as if he was in a nightmare.
Racked by the intrusive thoughts in his head that told him
he'd taken things a step too far.

She'd asked him to stay over. To spend Sunday with
her too. And though he could imagine it would be de-
lightful, and the babies would have fun, he knew he had
to think practically. Right now they were in a bubble. A
lovely bubble. One he would struggle to leave. But it was
the right thing to do.

He couldn't live in a bubble. He had to return to reality. Strong people, the people to admire, were the ones
who survived in harsh reality.

He couldn't stay here, warm and cosy, pressed up
against her body. Because already he was wanting more
of her, could feel his body awakened by its need to have
her again, But it would be wrong. He'd be taking advantage. Brooke had tried to put the brakes on last night and

she'd been right to do so. He ought to be the strong man she kept telling him he was and do something about it.

Gently he rolled away from her and slipped out of bed. He stood there for a moment to see if she would wake, and already he could feel his reluctance to leave. But, no.

I have to do this.

He padded softly away, wincing slightly as the door creaked, and crept into the lounge, where their clothes had been discarded the night before. He got dressed and hung her robe and long tee shirt over the back of the couch, neatly folded. Then he went into the other bedroom and grabbed the rest of his clothes and checked on Lily. She was starting to stir. Snuffling and rubbing at her face with her hands.

Matt checked the time. Six-thirty a.m. Lily was right on cue. He had no idea what time Brooke and Morgan would wake, but if he had the nerve to wait and let Lily wake on her own then he would be able to get her out of here without her crying.

Back in the lounge, he found a notepad and pen by the phone and scribbled Brooke a note. He tried to make it sound friendly, and not as if he were rejecting her. Saying that he just needed to pop home, and as he'd woken early he'd decided to leave her to rest and sleep in on her day off before work tomorrow.

He read the note over and over, wondering if he'd pitched it right. It seemed okay to him, but he was very aware of the fact that Brooke felt men always rejected her, and he didn't want her to think the same of him.

They would be sensible. Sort this out. Work through it. Like adults.

They'd be able to do that, right?

He had to believe that they would.

CHAPTER EIGHT

HE'D SPENT SUNDAY trying to put the night he and Brooke had spent together out of his mind—but it had been impossible. All he'd been able to think of was the way she had felt, the way she had tasted, those little sounds she had made in the back of her throat as he had made love to her and how good it had made him feel to be wrapped in her arms.

It had been one hot night, and he knew it was a night that he would never forget.

He'd left his mobile phone at home and taken Lily out for their usual five-mile walk. He'd gone all touristy and caught the bus to Trafalgar Square. He and Lily had fed the pigeons, walked through Covent Garden and along the Embankment. They'd eaten out at a small family-friendly cafeteria, and then he'd taken her to a small park where there were baby swings and small slides for her to play on.

And all the time he had been looking at Lily, talking to her, laughing with her, he'd seen his wife looking at him out of her eyes and he'd felt terrible for moving on. Felt as if he was horribly leaving his wife behind.

They'd had so many dreams, he and Jen, for their future. And what had he done? Taken *her* old job, in *her* old department, in some kind of sad effort to be in the place where his wife had lived and worked so that somehow he could still stay connected to her. So that he could touch the things that she had touched, chat with the people who had become her work family, and so that he could meet the famous Dr Brooke Bailey, whom he'd heard so much about and who was owed a promise.

I think I might have taken that promise too far.

And now he was at work early, waiting for his shift to start and fanning through the pages of the most recent medical journal.

There were some cutting edge developments happening in the world of medicine. On every page was evidence of people moving forward. Doctors and professors looking to see how they could improve things for the future. They weren't sitting still, being static. They knew that to improve you had to change with the times. Take risks.

And when he came to the back of the journal, where all the job vacancies were, his eyes were drawn to one in particular.

Auckland City Hospital.

Auckland, New Zealand. The place where he and Jen had planned to go in the future. The city that had been their ultimate goal—a place to raise their daughter. A place where Jen had spent time during her gap year and had loved.

But would considering something like that now be a move forward or a move backwards? It was an old dream. A dream that he'd shared with his wife.

She wasn't here any more and he was. And although they'd spent many a time talking about how wonderful it would be for their daughter, would doing it now, applying for the post, be the best thing for Lily? Jen had promised

Brooke that she would be there to help her raise Morgan, but she'd also wanted to emigrate. To do what was best for *their* little family. Shouldn't that be his priority?

He'd taken this job to put down roots. He wanted the future to be stable for Lily. She'd already lost her mother—did she need to be moved from pillar to post? Never quite sure where her home was? It wasn't a simple case of packing up your things and jumping on a plane. It meant leaving people behind. Leaving behind a life he'd already started to create and never planning for the future.

He'd had that sort of childhood, following his father in his postings abroad. Sometimes he'd liked it—other times he'd hated it. But he had grown to love it. Had matured and chosen the same life for himself. Had enrolled as a doctor in the army and flitted around the globe whilst Jen had stayed rooted in one spot.

Was it the right thing to do?

'Looking for another job?' asked Kelly as she glanced over his shoulder, walking to her locker and removing her coat and scarf. 'Have we driven you crazy so soon?'

He stared at the advertisement and grimaced. 'Not sure...'

Kelly hung up her things and then grabbed her stethoscope, draping it around her neck, then her ID card to pin to the waistband of her skirt. She came over and sat beside him, glancing at the advert. 'New Zealand? Beautiful place.'

'You've been there?'

'No. But I've always wanted to.' She took the magazine from him and smiled. 'Perhaps I ought to apply? Give you some competition.'

He laughed. 'I don't know what to do. Jen and I always

said that that's where we'd end up working. We wanted to give Lily an amazing life in a brand-new beautiful country.'

Kelly nodded. 'And it would be. Do it now—whilst she's a baby—and she'll probably never even remember the UK.'

Hmm… He'd not thought about that part. She *wouldn't* remember, would she? But *he* would. And he'd never forget all the wonderful people he had met here. His friends and his family were all here. And he'd be leaving behind Brooke.

That would be hard. Reneging on a promise.

He tossed the journal onto the table. 'It was just a thought. Anyway, are you trying to get rid of me, Kelly?' he asked with a smile.

'Gawd, no! You're the only decent thing to look at around here. If you left I don't know what I'd do!' She got up to make herself a quick cup of tea, and as she stood by the kettle raised an empty mug. 'Want one?'

'Sure.'

At that moment Brooke walked in, her face stony, and headed straight to her locker.

Matt got up and went over to her. 'Hi.'

She didn't look at him. She yanked open her locker and shrugged off her coat, then got out all the accoutrements she'd need for the day. She closed her locker and walked out again, without saying a word.

He watched her go, feeling awful inside. Perhaps he hadn't pitched his note as well as he'd thought? And perhaps leaving his phone behind all day on Sunday had not been a good idea either, because when he'd got back he'd seen missed calls and texts from Brooke, clearly wanting to talk to him.

Which he'd never answered.

'What did you *do*?' asked Kelly. 'If looks could've killed you'd be lying on a mortuary slab right now.'

'Looks like I need to apologise.' He put his hands in his pockets as he thought about how best to do that.

Kelly handed him his mug of tea. 'Well, I sure as hell hope you're good at grovelling, because that girl looked like she meant business.'

He sipped his tea and was thoughtful.

There was a hell of a lot he needed to think through today.

Brooke couldn't believe it! That he'd just said *hi* to her as if everything was okay between them! As if he hadn't walked out on her like that and left a stupid note.

He'd said that he would spend the day with them on Sunday. She'd made plans in her head—a walk in the park, maybe a meal out, a good chat over some good comfort food, maybe taking some pictures of the babies together—something like that. Nothing special. Just things they could do together.

But then they'd made love—unexpectedly—and it had been the single most amazing thing that had ever happened to her. No man had ever made her feel that way. It had been as if…as if…

As if he loved me…

That *had* to be wrong, right?

But the way he'd made love to her… That couldn't have been just sex. It hadn't been just a quickie—wham, bam, thank you, ma'am. It had been *special*. Tender. Loving. She'd felt as if she'd found the lost part of herself, one she'd never known was missing.

Falling asleep in his arms, in her bed, had felt *so good*. To know that he was wrapped around her, the length of his strong body against hers, had made her feel safe and secure for the first time since *for ever*.

The scent of him, the feel of his hard body moulded around hers...

She'd woken with a smile upon her face. A silly, dreamy smile as she'd yawned and stretched—and suddenly realised that there was no one next to her.

Brooke had sat up, alert, feeling the sheets to see if they were warm, to see if maybe she had dreamed it all. The sheets had been cold and she'd been naked, and she never slept naked, and her body had felt pleasantly used. As if she were glowing.

She'd thought that maybe he was in the kitchen. Or perhaps he'd had to get up to check on Lily in the next room?

So she'd lain back in bed against the pillows, still with a smile upon her face, thinking that at any minute he would come through the door and say good morning, and maybe—just maybe—if the babies weren't yet awake, have a repeat of what had happened last night?

She'd felt glad that they had come together. She'd had no regrets. Not then. Because she'd felt sure that of all the men in the world Matt was not one of those who would walk away from her and leave her behind. And they'd moved forward in their relationship, hadn't they? You didn't have a night like that with someone and walk away.

But she'd waited, and she'd waited, and when she'd started to get that funny feeling in her stomach she'd got up and slipped on a tee shirt and knickers to go and look for him.

And discovered that the only thing left of Matt and Lily was a note.

Brooke,

I'm sorry, but I had to go. We crossed a line last night, and I should never have allowed it to happen.

I didn't want to wake you. I know you offered for us to spend the day with you and Morgan, but I really think we should respect each other's boundaries, so I'll see you at work on Monday.

Many thanks once again,

Matt x

Many thanks? That was the response she got after what they had shared? *Many thanks?*

It was insulting. She'd tried to call him on his mobile, but it had just kept going to voicemail. She'd messaged him. Once. Then a second time. Then she'd worried that she might seem like some sort of obsessive stalker, so she'd stopped.

He would ring *her*, right? Surely it had *meant something* to him? Yes, they had crossed a line, but they had both wanted to. Hadn't they...?

But perhaps to him it hadn't meant anything at all? Perhaps she'd misread what was happening between them. And maybe she, so desperate for love and attention had mistaken his kindness for something more? To be left again like this was just so...painful.

When his silence had continued she'd got angrier and angrier that he'd apparently just dropped her like a hot potato after getting her into bed.

She was horrified that he could do that to her. Appalled. Aggrieved. Upset.

I've been used. He needed physical comfort and used me. Like I've always been used.

She wasn't sure she had anything to say to him. How

could he treat her like that after she'd told him how her dad had been with her? How Eric had been with her.

Brooke wasn't sure whether she wanted to rage at him, slap him across the face, or just never speak to him again. And his guilt had made her think of her own. Sleeping with Jen's husband, of all things! What had she been *thinking*?

But they had to work together. They had to be a team if the department was to run smoothly. So she'd thought the best way to be would be to say nothing at all. Not until the right moment presented itself. *Then* she would have something to say.

So she'd gone straight to work. Determined to fill her day with patient after patient after patient. With no more need to check in with Major Galloway she could get through her day without having to interact with him at all.

'Sarah Greenwood?' Brooke called for her first patient of the day.

A middle-aged woman stood up and followed her through to a cubicle.

'Hello, Miss Greenwood, my name's Dr Bailey. What can I do for you today?'

'I've been having these really bad abdominal pains. Like there's something trying to burst out of me. I feel… *full*. Bloated. It's horrible.'

'And how long have you been feeling like this?'

'A couple of weeks…I tried to call my GP to get an appointment, but I can't get in till near Christmas! I'm sorry, but I just had to come here—just to put my mind at rest if nothing else.'

'Okay. What type of pain is it? Is it a dull pain or a sharp one?'

Sarah shrugged. 'Both. It depends, sometimes, on what I'm doing.'

'And when was your last period?'

'Middle of October.'

'And is the pain all over, or just in one particular area?'

'It seems to be more on the left side.'

Knowing it could be any number of things, Brooke took Sarah's blood pressure, her temperature and her pulse. All seemed normal. 'Is there a chance that you could be pregnant?'

Sarah shook her head. 'No. I'm not with anybody right now.'

'No casual partners?'

'No.'

'When was the last time you had sex?'

Her patient blushed. 'Over a year ago.'

'Can I have a feel of your tummy?'

Sarah lay down on the bed and Brooke gave her a thorough examination of the abdomen. She thought she could feel a swelling on her patient's left side, possibly on her ovary, but she'd need an ultrasound to be sure.

'You can sit up now. Okay, Miss Greenwood, I'm not sure what this is, so I'll need to run a few more tests. Maybe get an ultrasound done—have you had one of those before?'

'No, but I know what they are. What do you think it is?'

'It could be several things at this stage. Let's do the ultrasound and see what happens. But don't worry—you're here now. I'll look after you.'

'I'm just worried that it's something serious. My mum had ovarian cancer, you see, and she started off the same way. I want to have children. I'm still young enough. And if it's something serious…'

The patient's family history was important, and it did not bode well. But that did not mean Sarah had ovarian cancer. It might be an ovarian cyst, which was often something simple to sort out.

'Do you have children, Doctor?'

Brooke nodded. 'I have a daughter.'

'You're lucky. I haven't found anyone yet who wants to stick around long enough to have children with me.'

Technically, neither had Brooke. Eric had been useless, and Matt... Well, she'd begun to think that he was the solid, dependable type, but she'd been wrong. Perhaps her radar was off? How had she managed to find men like that time after time? Did she have a big sign pointing at her head that read *'Needy and naïve'*?

'I worry I've left it too late, and now this...'

Brooke laid a reassuring hand on her patient's. 'Let's see what the tests say. It's way too early for you to be worrying before the results are in. I'm going to take a blood sample, too. Just to check and make sure there are no STDs.'

'Oh, I don't think I've got anything like that—'

'You'd be surprised, sometimes. Did you always use protection the last time you had a sexual partner?'

'Not every time, no.'

'And were you exclusive?'

She grimaced. '*I* was.'

Brooke smiled in sympathy. 'I'm sorry. So let's check that out anyway. I'll be back in a tick.'

'Thank you, Doctor.'

Brooke headed off to get a kit that would allow her to take blood, and also to ask one of the healthcare assistants to bring the portable ultrasound to her cubicle when it was next free.

'Dr Bailey?'

Hearing Matt's voice, she closed her eyes, telling her-

self silently to remain calm. She opened them again and
turned around. 'Yes?'

'Could I have a moment of your time to talk to you?'

'I'm busy with a patient right now.'

'It's important.'

'My patient is important, Major Galloway. Now, if
you'll excuse me?'

And she headed back, proud of herself for staying
calm and polite and for not having looked at him. Because if she had she might have faltered. And she wanted
to remain angry right now. It helped. Somehow…

She took Sarah's blood and then performed the ultrasound, moving the Doppler over her patient's abdomen
and soon noting a large cyst on the left ovary. It looked
benign, filled with fluid, but due to the patient's history
it needed to be checked and tested to be on the safe side.
It might burst on its own in time, or be reabsorbed, but
it might have been there for a while. Sarah would need
to see a specialist for further tests they just couldn't do
in A&E at this time.

Brooke explained the situation and promised to write
to her GP to arrange the referral. 'Try not to worry, Miss
Greenwood.'

'Thank you, I'll try. But I can't promise. Not until I
know for sure.'

'I understand. Take care.' And she waved her patient
goodbye.

She went back to write up her notes. As she did so
Matt came striding out of Majors, with Kelly following
behind him.

'Dr Bailey, I need you to come with us for a major incident. There's been a large traffic collision just down
the road and there are people trapped in vehicles. The
paramedic on scene has requested doctors.'

'There are none on scene?'

'All mobile doctors and the HEMS crew are busy on other cases, and the advanced paramedics have been called to another incident ten miles away. We're the closest, and you and Kelly are the most experienced on my team.'

'Okay.' She'd been called out on a field team twice before. Once to the London bus bombings some years before, and a second time to a train crash. Both times had been horrendous.

She hurried to grab the jacket that would identify her as a doctor at the scene, grabbed the kit bags that were always ready and prepped for occasions such as this, and quickly hurried after Matt and Kelly.

They were taken to the RRV—rapid response vehicle—that would drive them to the scene.

Her thoughts were whizzing like mad as they negotiated their way through the thick traffic that had built up. It was agonising to sit there, inching forward like a snail. She almost felt as if it would be faster to get out and run, but then suddenly the cars parted and they could get through, and they arrived to find a refuse collection lorry had crashed through a car, up a pathway and into a café.

There was smashed glass everywhere, alarms were going off, and people were crying, looking horrified. Sickeningly, she spotted one or two people with their mobile phones out, filming it all or taking pictures.

But she had no time to worry about them. That was for the police to take care of. *She* was here for the casualties.

A fire engine was already there, and a fireman in a white helmet, indicating his high rank, was letting them in on who their casualties were.

'The driver of the lorry had a heart attack at the wheel. My guys have been giving CPR, but there's been no sign of life now for over twenty minutes. There were two other men in the truck, both have cuts and lacerations. The driver of the car that was smashed up is trapped within the vehicle and we're working to free her. There are also numerous casualties in the café, including a pregnant woman who has taken a blow to the abdomen. Multiple lacerations throughout, and we have victims in shock. One customer of the café was knocked down by the truck as it entered the building and appears to have broken his leg.'

Matt nodded. 'I'll take the guy in the truck. Dr Bailey, if you could handle the driver of the car and, Kelly, you check out the café customers. Triage only. Understood? I'll join you as soon as I can.'

They all nodded and headed off to deal with their patients.

Brooke made her way to the smashed up car, its bonnet crumpled and steaming, watching whilst firefighters tried to remove the roof. A fireman sat in the back seat, holding the driver's head still.

'What's the patient's name?'

'Vijaya.'

'Okay.' She removed a cervical collar from her kit, ready to attach it to the patient's neck. 'Vijaya? My name's Brooke and I'm a doctor from the London Grace. Are you in any pain?'

'My neck hurts—and my leg.'

'Okay… Well, you've got a handsome fireman holding your spine nice and straight for me, and I'm just going to have a quick feel of your neck before I put this collar on. I want you to tell me if anything hurts.'

With her fingers she probed Vijaya's neck, feeling along the vertebrae. 'Anything?'

'I don't know. It just hurts.'

'Were you stationary when the lorry hit you?'

'Yes. I'd just got in…was about to pull away. I'd just released the handbrake when the lorry hit me.'

'I'm going to check out the rest of you, if I can.' Brooke made a primary survey—checking for breaks, bleeds, anything obvious. 'Does your chest hurt?'

'A little.'

'Did you have your seatbelt on?'

'Yes.'

'And how does your breathing feel? Does it hurt to breathe in?'

'No.'

'Take a deep breath for me.'

Vijaya did so. 'It doesn't hurt.'

That was good. Brooke peered in as far as she could and saw that the engine block had been pushed in somewhat, and was pinning Vijaya's left leg. There was some bleeding.

'Can you wiggle your toes for me?'

'Yes.'

'You can feel both feet?'

'Yes. My leg hurts, though.'

'Your leg seems trapped, Vijaya. I don't know how badly you're injured—we won't know until we get you free. It shouldn't be long. Do you have any medical problems I need to know about?'

'I'm a Type Two diabetic.'

'Okay, anything else?'

'No. Well, I'm claustrophobic…'

Brooke could see the frantic look in Vijaya's eyes as the firemen put up a sheet to protect her from glass as they cut away the car's roof. Being trapped in the car with all these firemen about, and now the tarpaulin, must be very scary indeed.

She reached in and took Vijaya's hand in hers. 'I've

got you. Just a moment or two more. Do you have any family I can call?'

'My husband is probably wondering where I am.'

'What's his name?'

'Rav.'

'And his number?' With her free hand she pulled out her mobile and as Vijaya told them to her punched in the digits and listened to the phone ringing at the other end. 'He's not answering. I'll try again in a minute.'

The firemen suddenly lifted off the roof of the car and Brooke went round to the other side of the vehicle to try and get a better look at Vijaya's leg. She couldn't be sure, but she didn't think there was too much damage. It looked like a simple entrapment. The wound would need cleaning, an X-ray to check for any bone damage and possibly a few stitches. It was her patient's neck she was more worried about.

As the firemen worked to free her patient's leg, Brooke became aware of Matt at her side. 'Can you give me an update?'

Brooke gave details of her patient to Matt, being as robotic as she could, because right now, her anger and her upset had to wait. Matt nodded and then ran to check on Kelly. She watched him go, registering a look in his eyes that she had never seen before. But she guessed he must be used to scenes of such carnage. This sort of thing didn't faze him. He had a place in his head he could go to that allowed him to keep a professional distance and look past the screams, the yells, and see what needed to be done in the most efficient manner he could.

In moments he'd left Kelly and nipped into the café's interior, where she lost sight of him.

He was a good doctor. He really was. And she'd

thought he was a good man. One whom she could finally lean upon.

I should have known better.

The firemen freed Vijaya's leg quickly, and as a team they managed to get her onto a back board and lift her free of the vehicle. Brooke attended to the wound on her patient's leg, applying a dressing quickly to prevent further blood loss, knowing that she would get full treatment soon in an A&E.

She clutched Vijaya's hand one more time. 'You're going in an ambulance now. I've got to stay here to help more patients, but I'll come and check on you when I get back.'

'Which hospital am I going to?'

'The London Grace.'

'Oh. Right.'

'I'll see you there.'

She picked up her kit bag, disposed of her gloves and put on fresh ones, and then ran into the café to assist Matt.

She was like a bee. Flitting from patient to patient, assessing, dressing wounds, giving reassuring smiles and holding the hands of those who were wounded or frightened.

Matt watched her, glad that he had picked her for his field team, still hoping that she would give him the chance to explain himself.

He'd hurt her. He knew that. And that did not sit well with him. He was not the kind of guy to walk over someone else's feelings and it unsettled him.

He finished applying a splint to the patient with a broken leg and got him onto a spinal board for transport to an ambulance. He held the patient's hand as he walked alongside the trolley to the vehicle and he was smiling when he heard an almighty rumble and turned to see what the noise was.

The front of the café was obscured by a thick dust cloud and rubble lay all around. *Had the front of the café collapsed?* He saw, to his left, Kelly clambering out of the back of an ambulance. Was Brooke still inside?

He ran over to the front of the café, but a fireman held him back. 'You can't go in—it's not stable.'

'I've got a doctor inside!'

'We need to stabilise the area. Stand back.'

The firemen pushed him back, away from the frontage of the building. All he could think about were the people inside. The patients. *Brooke!* How close had she been to the front of the café? Was she under the rubble? Was she hurt?

Was he ever going to see her again and get the chance to say he was sorry?

I need to get in!

He made to dart forward, but the firemen had been watching him and placed a solid hand upon his chest. 'Stay right where you are.'

It took far too long for the firemen to put up joists and clear the rubble but finally, when the moment came and they allowed him in, he rushed forward, desperate to make sure that Brooke was okay.

He was met by a stream of walking wounded who were all clambering out into the light. He helped them all, his mind going crazy, before he was able to clamber over the debris to find Brooke—packing up her kit bag and hauling it over her shoulder.

The relief he felt was palpable. 'You're okay. Thank God.'

She looked at him, seemed slightly shocked, but nodded. 'I'm fine.'

'When the front of the café fell in I...' He swallowed. 'But you're okay. That's what matters.'

'I'm all right.'

'When we get back you and me are going to have that talk.'

'I'm tired, Matt, and I need a drink. Maybe a shower. I'm covered in dust.'

'Okay. But afterwards?'

She nodded. 'Afterwards.'

He pulled her kit bag from her shoulder and slung it over his, then took her hand, to her surprise, and led her safely out over the rubble.

Blinking again at the brightness, Brooke pulled her hand free of his and headed back to the RRV. Kelly got in beside her and he saw them exchange looks.

He got into the front and sat beside the driver. 'You did a great job—both of you.'

'Thanks.'

'There was just the one fatality. The lorry driver. I think he had a massive MI.'

The driver's myocardial infarction—heart attack— must have been instantaneous, and unfortunately, he'd been driving a large, powerful vehicle that had spun out of control.

You never knew when your time would come. Matt had once thought *his* time had come in Khost Province. Had been sure that at any moment he would be struck down. But he'd survived. Survived to become a father. To know his daughter. To know Brooke. And she was special. And he didn't want to waste all the good opportunities he had in life and make people miserable.

He'd lost his wife unexpectedly.

Did he really want to lose Brooke, too?

CHAPTER NINE

His mind was in turmoil. Now that the adrenaline had gone—now that he was thinking rationally as he waited for Brooke to get out of the hospital's showers—he began seriously to analyse just how he'd felt when the frontage of that café had collapsed.

How had it come to be that he had allowed himself to develop feelings for another woman? And so deeply? Okay, so he'd never told himself that he wouldn't get involved again after Jen. He'd never said that. He'd known there might be the possibility at *some point* that someone might come along. He'd just never expected it this soon. And he'd certainly never expected it to be his wife's best friend.

He'd assumed it would be someone a long time in the future—when Lily was a teenager, maybe.

But for it to have happened this fast... That was what he was having trouble with.

Because when the front of that café had collapsed his heart had almost stopped. The horror, the dread that had filled him at the idea that Brooke was trapped, or hurt, or even dead under that rubble, had almost killed *him*, too. That another woman he cared for could be cruelly taken from him without warning... *Again*...

Matt looked down at the table and saw the journal

he'd been looking at earlier. It was still open at the page he'd left it. The tantalising possibility of a job at Auckland City Hospital.

It was an amazing opportunity. Fortuitous. Something he'd once dreamed of going for. Moving Lily to New Zealand would give her an amazing life, but no matter what he decided he would always put the welfare of his little girl first.

So what *was* best for her? The new life he and Jen had always wanted? Or staying here, where life was getting complicated? Could he have Brooke enter his life so deeply and be so integrated into it that Lily might call her *Mama?*

The thought of that made him feel terrible. Not because Brooke would be a bad role model as a mother. She was an excellent mum to her own daughter. But he wasn't sure he could cope with having his daughter call Brooke *Mum*. It felt treacherous.

He'd imagined raising his little girl and sitting her on his knee, getting out the photo albums and showing her pictures of her mummy and telling her all about Jen. About how like Jen she was. About how much they looked alike and how much her mother had loved her. He needed Lily to know that. And if Brooke was in their lives would that make things more complicated?

He picked up the journal and looked at it once again. Read through the job description, the requirements, the contact details...

Perhaps I need to keep my options open? I could just ring them for a quick chat. I could just see what it would all be about.

Yes, if he went to New Zealand he'd be leaving Brooke and everyone here behind, but perhaps that was what they needed? A fresh start. By staying he had enveloped himself in *Jen's* past, not his own. He had come here in an effort to know her better, to meet those who had loved her, in an attempt to keep her alive in his head. Getting involved with Brooke had been wrong. He'd lost his focus in a moment of lust and his feelings for his wife's best friend were strong now. He wasn't sure he should be feeling that way.

It was entirely possible that going to New Zealand would also be the wrong thing to do. He couldn't live Jen's life. He had to live his own. But his own life had also included the aspiration to move to New Zealand. To emigrate. To give his daughter a bright future in an amazing country. It was all so confusing.

Matt headed to his office and closed the door. He picked up the phone and called the number. He wasn't sure of the time difference, or even if anyone would answer, but he figured he could leave his details and ask them to email him.

But someone answered.

An actual person.

And so he began his enquiries about the vacancy.

The shower felt great. To just stand there motionless, letting the hot spray hit her body, her head, her shoulders, her back, feeling it washing away the dust and debris… pounding sore muscles that were still recovering from the adrenaline rush that had smothered her when the front wall of the café had collapsed.

For a moment she had thought she would die.

She'd been helping a patient, wrapping gauze around a penetrative leg injury, when she'd heard a strange creak and a groan. As if the world itself was about to crumble. And then it had felt as if the sky had fallen as the front of the café had come crashing down, filling her lungs with dust and grit as everything went dark.

She'd leaned over her patient, protecting her, covering her own head and hoping that somehow she would survive.

The only thought in her head had been *Morgan!*

Her little girl. In the hospital crèche, probably playing happily with something, or sitting in a puddle of paint, smiling, laughing. She could lose her mother at any minute. Morgan might have to grow without a mother as well as without a father.

Who would care for her?

Not her dad. Social services would never give a baby to a drunk. So that just left Eric, Morgan's father, and there was no way she would want that. And there was no way *he'd* want the intrusion of his child turning up in his sad little life.

And then she'd thought of poor Lily, who actually had no mother but did have a loving, kind father, and she'd begun to wonder, as she coughed dirt and dust from her lungs and wiped the grime from her face, whether she had misjudged Matt?

He wasn't a bad guy. She knew that. Deep down. He was a brilliant doctor. Kind and caring. Professional. He ran the A&E department beautifully. It had never been as efficient as it was now, under his leadership. And as a father, he was top notch. She saw it in his face whenever he collected his daughter at the end of the day. Just how much he'd missed her was in his eyes. In the way he would pull her towards him and breathe in the scent of her hair and kiss her. He was determined to be everything his little girl needed now that she was motherless.

And that night they'd spent together... Cads and users didn't make love to a woman like that. It had been

more than sex, she was sure of it, so why had he walked
away? And if he *was* a user of women—which she now
doubted—he would never have left a note, would he? He
would have just walked out. And, okay, he hadn't answered her text messages or phone calls, but she had no
idea what had happened to him after he'd left her flat.

She owed him the opportunity—his chance to explain.
Because life was too short to waste it on petty grievances.
Matt was not her father. He wasn't Eric. And he deserved
his chance to speak.

Switching off the shower, she got dressed and dried
her hair, sweeping it up into a ponytail and then went to
find him.

He was in his office, on the phone. His gaze met hers
as she stood in the doorway and he held up his hand as
if to say *two minutes.*

She nodded, happy to wait, and sat in the chair opposite, trying not to listen in but hearing words like *New
Zealand* and *emigrating* and wondering who on earth he
could be talking to.

Eventually he put down the phone and looked her over.
Then he smiled, as if he was happy to see she had no cuts,
no bruises, no injuries.

'You're okay?' he asked.

She nodded. 'I am. A little weary, but good.'

'I'm glad to hear it. When I saw what had happened I
didn't know what to think.'

She gave him a polite smile, acknowledging his worry
about her wellbeing. 'What happened, Matt?'

'The front of the café collap—'

'No. After our night together. You just left. You never
answered my calls.'

He had the decency to look appalled with himself.
'I'm sorry. Did you see my note?'

Unfortunately. 'Yes.'

'I did want to stay with you. Spend the day with you, like we'd planned, but...'

'But?'

'I've not been with a woman since Jen died. I hadn't expected to be with a woman like that for a long time. And yet somehow there I was, in your bed, with you in my arms, and it felt *so right*... But I felt guilty. Terribly guilty. I don't know...it was a knee-jerk reaction, and I justified it to myself by thinking that I needed a shower and a change of clothes, and that I didn't want to monopolise your whole weekend...I'm sorry. It's not a good enough excuse. It was an instinctual thing. I just left. It was wrong of me.'

'And you didn't answer my messages.'

'I left my phone behind and went out for the whole day. I felt like I owed it to Lily—as if I'd betrayed her mother's memory and I owed it to her. It was no slight on you. What we had was...'

She waited to hear how he'd describe their night together. Hoping that he would confirm to her that he had felt the same way. That they'd discovered a deep connection between them...that it had been more than just sex. More than just a cheap night—something passionate and intimate and loving.

'Just magical.'

She allowed herself a small smile. So he *had* felt it too. That was good. She hadn't been imagining things. 'It meant something. Didn't it?'

'More than I suspected it would.'

Her smile broadened. 'What happened today at the café, when the roof came in. I thought that...I thought I might die. I'm not trying to be dramatic, but it made me think about life and how short it is. We've both lost Jen. I thought Morgan might lose me as well.'

'*I* would have lost you, too.'

She nodded. *Yes.* They'd both been hit by the events of today. 'I didn't want to waste any more time on being angry with you. That night showed me that we could have something special.'

'Brooke—'

'Let me finish. Please.' She leaned forward. 'You *mean* something to me. I never expected it. I never thought for a moment that I would feel this way about you. But I do, and I think if we're offered the chance of happiness in our lives we should take it.' She smiled. 'I don't often put myself out on the line like this. I don't declare my feelings. But I'd like to think that if you feel the same way about me as I do about you then we should embrace that.'

Her stomach was rolling as she spoke. Butterflies in their thousands were flitting around in her insides as she waited for his response. She hoped he would smile. Hoped he would come out from behind the desk and take her in his arms and hold her tight. Press her up against his body and whisper into her hair that he loved her.

But he remained seated behind his desk. His face was a mass of conflicting emotions. 'We *should* take chances—you're right. It's too easy to stay in our comfort zones, wrapping ourselves up in the familiar. We *should* take chances.'

She might be wrong, but she felt as if he was saying that to himself, rather than to her. Perhaps he was trying to persuade himself? He'd admitted to feeling guilty about what they'd shared, and she could understand that. It wasn't that long ago that his wife had died, and perhaps he was struggling with that more than she knew? Perhaps he needed a little extra time to get used to this change? To accept the fact that she had feelings for him and wanted to pursue a relationship with him.

Because she absolutely did. She might have been burned by men in the past, but the way she felt about Matt… She absolutely felt sure that he was worth it. That by putting her cards on the table she was making herself vulnerable, yes, but she was also being brave. She wasn't going to let her past dictate her future. She was going to take a chance on love *despite* that.

She'd thought she might die today. And she would have died without letting Matt know how she really felt. He needed to know. Anybody who loved needed to let the person they cherished understand just how they felt. It was an important thing to hear. Words had power. Magic. It wasn't just actions that proved how you felt.

Brooke decided to give him some time to digest what she'd said. 'I'm just going to go check on Morgan before I return to work, if that's okay?'

He looked up at her as if he'd been lost in his own thoughts. 'What? Oh, right. Yes. Sure…'

She headed to the door, and then a thought occurred to her. 'Earlier, when I first came in, you were talking on the phone about emigration… New Zealand. What was that about? Have we got a new doctor joining us?'

His face coloured. 'No. I…I was just chatting to a colleague who's thinking of going. Making a new life out there.'

'Oh. Sounds wonderful. I've heard it's beautiful out there. I think Jen mentioned it once.'

He nodded, his face stern.

'Well, I'll see you later, then?'

'Yes.'

She smiled a goodbye and left his office. He was clearly stunned by what she'd said. Surprised at the depth of her feelings for him. But it was important to her to be honest with him. Then there'd be no surprises, no disappointments. If he didn't feel the same way then she would hurt for a while, but she would get over it. In time. And she would know that she had been honest and open, and that was what was important. Honesty. Truth.

Because if you didn't have that then there was no point in having anything at all.

Morgan's face lit up at the sight of her mummy's unexpected visit. She raised her arms, asking to be picked up, and Brooke scooped her up and held her tight, kissing her cheeks and just breathing her in.

She stayed with her for a while, watching her play with pasta shapes, squealing and burbling, making all her happy sounds, picking up a particular piece she wanted to show her mummy and beaming when Brooke made a happy face.

Moments like these were precious. Watching her daughter made Brooke realise just how much she was missing out on. Morgan had long days here in the crèche. Ten hours every day. Monday to Friday. That was fifty hours a week that she didn't get to spend with her child. Morgan was growing quickly, developing at a breakneck pace, and she was missing it.

When she'd left Morgan at the crèche that morning it had been no big deal. She'd dropped her off, given her one last kiss and then walked away, sure that in ten hours she would see her again. No biggie.

Only she might have died today and she'd been so *nonchalant* about leaving her child. Had taken no time to breathe in her scent, to give her one last hug, to tell her that she loved her.

These early days were important and she was missing them—crossing off the days of her calendar at work instead of by her daughter's side.

Matt wasn't the only one who suffered from guilt. She did, too. It was something she would have to think about.

So she kissed her daughter goodbye, breathed in the scent of her daughter's hair and gave her one last hug before she returned to work. Maybe she could claim a week's holiday? Spend it at home with Morgan. Some of it with Matt, perhaps. Take some time out together to just *be*.

Entering A&E, she saw Kelly give her a wave, and as Kelly had been at the accident site this morning with her and Matt she went to give her friend a hug.

'Hey, what's that for?' Kelly asked, surprised.

'Just a hug to say I appreciate you. That I love you.'

'Aw, thanks. I love you, too.'

Brooke smiled. 'Crazy start to the day, huh?'

'You're telling me. But it was thrilling to get out into the field. We don't often get that opportunity. It was good to see the paramedics' side of it.'

Brooke nodded. That was true. The guys in green brought in the majority of their patients, and she was so used to them just turning up with people on stretchers or backboards it didn't occur to her to think about the sights they saw during the course of their working day.

'True.'

'I think it's good to have change, don't you? Keeps you fresh. Keeps you on your toes.'

'I think you're right.'

'I believe our Major is looking for change, too.'

Brooke frowned. 'What do you mean?'

'He was looking at a new job opportunity this morning. In New Zealand, of all places! You can't get more of a change than that.'

She felt her blood run cold as she began to understand. '*He* wants to go to New Zealand?'

'That's what he said. We'll miss him here, but I wouldn't blame him for going and giving it a try.'

Brooke's heart pounded fast and heavy in her chest as all sound around her seemed to grow fuzzy and indistinct. She became incredibly aware of each breath, her gaze dropping to the floor as she fought just to stay upright.

He lied to me!

She'd asked him outright! After all that had happened that morning—the collapse of the café, how close she had come to losing her life—the first thing he'd done was enquire about a job on the other side of the world?

Perhaps I don't mean anything to him at all!

'Brooke? You okay? You've gone very pale.'

'I…I don't feel very well.'

'Sit down for a minute.' Kelly pulled out a chair.

'No. I think I need to go home. It's nearly the end of my shift anyway. I'm going to go pick up Morgan. I need to be with her. Spend time with her. With the people who love me back.'

And she hurriedly began to walk away.

As each step took her further and further away from A&E her anger and despair rose inside her, and she fought back tears as she smacked the button to call for the lift. *Why?* Why had he outright *lied*? She'd laid herself bare before him and he'd lied. That he could do that to her, when she'd exposed herself like that…made herself open and vulnerable…

At the crèche, Daisy looked surprised to see her again so quickly. 'Dr Bailey! Everything okay?'

'I've come to collect Morgan. I… We need to go home.'

'Oh, okay. I've just put her down for a nap. Should I wake her?'

'Yes. Please. Hurry.'

'Of course.' Daisy scurried away.

Brooke stood there waiting, feeling humiliated beyond belief.

How many times would a man stamp all over her heart?

How many times would she allow that to happen?

Not any more.

Never, ever again!

Matt hammered on Brooke's front door. 'Brooke? Brooke, it's me. Please, would you just open the door and let me in? We need to talk.' He banged on the door again.

Behind him a door opened and the occupant came out. It was a young man wearing very loose jogging bottoms and a black vest, showing his perfectly honed gym body to perfection. 'Dude? What's with the noise? I'm trying to sleep in here.'

Matt looked at him, irritated. 'It's four o clock in the afternoon.'

'You never heard of night shifts? Brooke's at work. She works every day.'

'She came home. I know she's in there.'

'Well, she's not the type to ignore people, so you must have upset her big-time, dude.'

'Thank you for that observation.' Exasperated, Matt closed his eyes and turned back to hammer on Brooke's door.

Behind him, the man closed his door. Matt knelt down and opened Brooke's letterbox. 'Brooke? Please let me in! I'm disturbing the neighbours and I know you don't want me to—'

The door was yanked open and he almost fell forward. But he instantly got to his feet and stared at the woman he had too many feelings for.

'I'm sorry.'

'You say that a lot to me just recently. I'm not sure it means anything any more.'

'Can I please come in? Would you just give me a moment to explain?'

Brooke shook her head, tears glazing her eyes. 'No. You can't. I told you *everything*. Everything I felt. I laid myself bare to you. I gave you the opportunity to be truthful to me. But you lied. You want to go to New Zealand? Then you go, Matt. Don't you worry about me. I'll be fine.'

She went to close the door, but he blocked it with his foot.

'I wanted to tell you! I *did*! But I couldn't. Because if I had told you exactly how I feel then that would've made it real. If I'd told you that I love you then that would have been me closing the door on everything I had with Jen, and I couldn't do that. New Zealand was a dream. An escapist fantasy that I indulged in because I was afraid of what was happening between us! Don't you *see*?'

She stared down at his foot in disdain, then looked back up at him. 'No. You don't get to have the monopoly on being afraid! You think you're the only one? That because you've already lost one love you have the most to lose?'

She banged at his foot with the door.

'I lost her too! My best friend in the whole world! But you know what? I started to find another. I started to believe that this new friend was going to mean just as much. And I gave my heart willingly, only for it to be crushed— once again—by an unfeeling, inconsiderate coward who's afraid to admit how he feels! Now, you'd better remove that foot right now, or I'm going to go into my kitchen, find the sharpest knife I have and surgically remove it!'

She glared at him, tears and fury blurring her eyes, and he could do nothing but remove his foot and allow the door to be slammed in his face.

He stood there, momentarily stunned. Unsure of what to do. He didn't hear the door behind him open once again. Wasn't aware of the guy standing watching him, an amused smirk on his face, until he heard, 'Dude, you messed up.'

He closed his eyes, felt tears sting behind closed lids, and felt his heart break.

Brooke called in sick that first week. Then Personnel informed him that Brooke had taken some annual leave owed to her.

Matt sat in his office in between patients, feeling numb and broken. He'd made a big mess of everything. He had disrupted not only the department—because everyone wanted to know what was wrong with Brooke—but also his own life.

He was lost without her here. Not seeing her every day was torture, plain and simple.

He'd had fights with Jen, but nothing like this. Life seemed so bleak. He found it hard to smile. Found it hard to concentrate on what anyone was saying. Found himself drifting off into thoughts of that last argument as he sat in departmental meetings. He tried his hardest to find joy and smile and laugh when he was with Lily, but even she seemed subdued by his mood and cried a lot, constantly needing his hugs.

Hugging his daughter was the only thing that brought relief. He'd just sit and watch Lily playing on the carpet.

He *didn't* want to uproot them and take them to New Zealand. He'd panicked. Brooke was right on that score. He'd been scared. Scared of what his feelings for her meant. He'd lost control, just for a moment, and rung about that stupid job.

He should have told her about it from the beginning, but as he hadn't been definite about going he hadn't thought it was worth mentioning. It had been a blip. A small error in judgement as he'd frantically fought to regain control over his feelings. Because he'd felt as if they were running away from him. Like wild horses, their glorious manes flowing behind them as they ran across a grassy plain.

He'd tried to rein his feelings in, and he could see now that it had been the wrong thing to do. Because you couldn't rein in love. It was a wild thing. An uncontrollable animal that defied attempts to tame it. It would always be free. It demanded to be free. And accepting his feelings as truth was a big step for him.

He'd loved Jen. He would always love her. Every single day. But that love was not lessened by his love for Brooke. They were two separate things.

The fact that he still had the capacity to fall deeply in love had, at first been startling. But now it was painful. Because he'd screwed it up. He'd hurt the woman he loved and he didn't know how to fix it.

He'd tried apologising. He'd sent flowers. Had texted. Called. But she hadn't responded and he wasn't sure he could face the hurt of having her slam the door in his face yet again.

So he was giving her time. Because if he'd learned anything from Jen's death it was that time lessened the hurt. It didn't take it away. It didn't get rid of it completely. But you absorbed it better. It wasn't so raw and painful as it could be in the early days.

Time allowed you to take a deep breath and just *breathe*.

He was biding his time and hoping that maybe—just maybe—when she was ready to return to work she would let him tell her everything.

She had to return to work. Even if it was just to work out her notice.

So much had changed for her recently, and there'd been some startling revelations, but she knew she had to do what was right for her. And for Morgan. And...

Brooke closed her eyes and took a deep breath as she handed Morgan over to Daisy in the crèche. She wouldn't have to do this much longer. Not here, anyway.

Brooke had decided that what she and Morgan needed was a change and some rest. So she was taking a leaf out of Matt's book. She'd been rash before, hurrying back to work after her maternity leave, when she wasn't fully ready. And that rashness had caused her to do something silly. To fall in love with a man who was wholeheartedly unavailable.

She should have seen that—acknowledged that—but she'd been silly and allowed him into her heart. And, as in all the times before, in every single relationship she had ever had with a man, her feelings had been crushed.

But things were different now. She was taking back control. No longer a passive observer in her own life, letting things happen to her. *She* was going to be the one who made the changes. If Matt could consider going to New Zealand and leaving, then she could make huge changes too.

That meant putting in her notice, working it out, and

then she and Morgan were going to head to the south west coast for a while. Maybe Cornwall. She'd heard it was beautiful there. She was going to hire a mobile home and they'd pootle around the area for a few weeks whilst she waited to start the job that she'd accepted just yesterday.

She would be working at another A&E—far, far away from London and its great impersonal greyness. Its hustle and bustle. Its demand for you to hurry. For you to pay, pay, pay. It was a city in which you could lose yourself, and Brooke didn't want that. She wanted to relax more. To enjoy nature.

Her new job was in a town, yes, but the cottage that she'd seen was by the coast. It would be perfect to raise her children there. To live. To lie in bed and hear waves crashing against the beach. To hear the gulls. To take long walks along the coast, squeezing sand between her toes, watching her daughter and whoever was next to come sitting in the sand, making sandcastles…

Discovering she was carrying Matt's baby had come as a shock. They'd used protection, but she'd found herself one morning, peeing onto a stick and then watching the blue lines appear, bright as day.

How *could* she have got herself in the same mess she'd been in when she got pregnant with Morgan? Was she so naïve regarding her own feelings that she'd be one of those women with a brood of children, each of them with a different father?

She had no expectations of him. She could imagine his hurt, his pain at the prospect of a child who would become just another piece of evidence that he had somehow betrayed his wife.

I can't compete with a ghost.

She'd loved Jen so much! And she felt guilty to think that she was carrying her best friend's husband's child.

Even if a small part of her thought that Jen might be smiling at the development, up there in heaven. That Jen might even have plotted this herself!

Thrown you another curve ball, honey!

So Matt would receive two big pieces of news this morning.

She hoped he would be a big enough man to let her go. But another part of her hoped that somehow he might tell her everything she wanted to hear.

Miracles happened, didn't they? Wasn't she deserving of a turn at happiness? Hadn't she paid her dues? Finding out she was pregnant with Morgan had been a huge turning point in her life, and it was going to be the same with Matt's baby.

Now or never.

A new life was on its way. A new baby. Brooke had always wanted a family—a few kids, a husband. The perfect little unit.

So, okay, maybe life wanted to challenge her with this. Make her fight for what she needed. She'd never backed down from a fight. Had always stood her ground. Maybe she would get what she wanted some day, even if it wasn't now.

But she *would* get it.

She was determined.

CHAPTER TEN

MATT WAS IN his office. For a moment she watched him through the small window, saw the hunching of his shoulders, the lifeless look in his eyes as he stared numbly at a staffing rota.

She didn't normally like to see anyone hurting like that. But a tiny part of her was *glad* that it wasn't easy for him. Because she'd been feeling as if she was the only one suffering.

She rapped her knuckles on the door and he looked up, standing instantly, becoming alert when he saw who was standing there.

Brooke opened the door and went in. The envelope in her hand contained her notice. 'I've come to give you this.'

She passed it over and he took it from her with confusion, turning it over to see if the envelope gave any clue to its contents.

'What is it?'

'My notice.'

His face fell. 'Brooke, no…there's no need for that.'

'There's every need. I'll work my notice. I won't drop you in it by leaving you down a doctor.'

'Brooke—'

'I'm late. I need to get on.'

And she hurried out, her nerve failing her in delivering the extra bit of news that she knew would change everything. Handing in her notice and walking away was one thing. It showed courage and determination. Telling a man she was pregnant and having him want nothing to do with her turned the tables and would make her feel pathetic and alone. And she wasn't ready to face that just yet.

Maybe she could hold the news until her last day at work? She was in no hurry for him to reject her. She'd been there once before with Eric. She was in no rush to hear it a second time.

Even though she suspected Matt would probably want to do the right thing, him being the kind of person she knew him to be, a small part of her was worried that he would not. Lily was the most important thing in his world, and another baby, with another woman, was not ever going to be part of his life plan. It would throw him completely. And he would tear himself apart trying to do the honourable thing and yet also bear the weight of his betrayal to his wife.

She would wait. She still had time before there were any signs of her pregnancy.

Shoulders back, chin up, she grabbed the first patient's chart and headed back to work.

The letter was stark and to the point. She was leaving. Brooke was going to leave the London Grace!

Just the idea of that was...

He had no words for how it made him feel. His heart had jumped when he'd seen her at his office door. He'd been hoping that she had reconsidered. Was now willing to listen to his explanation. But she'd been brusque and kept their conversation short.

But she was here now. He had a month to get her to listen to him. And he didn't have to send her letter of notice up to Personnel just yet. He would hold on to it for a while.

Maybe he wouldn't be able to stop her from leaving, but he was determined that somehow he would get her to listen to him. Even if it changed nothing between them, he needed to tell her how he felt. How their relationship had blossomed into something that he'd never expected. How his feelings for her had grown into something he couldn't control and how that had made him feel.

Another knock on his door interrupted his thoughts and he stood up abruptly, hoping it might be Brooke. Only it wasn't. An old man stood there. A man who looked familiar.

'Arthur?'

It was Patricia's husband. The man who had brought in his wife after a stroke.

'You remember me?'

The old man shuffled in and Matt indicated that he should take a seat.

'Of course. How are you?'

Still reeling from Brooke's news, Matt forced himself to focus as he sank back into his chair.

'I wanted to come here to thank you, Doctor. You and your team.'

'Oh, well, there's no need—we were just doing our jobs. How is your wife?'

Arthur's eyes darkened slightly. 'She passed away a day or two after we returned her to the care home. It was peaceful. Her funeral was yesterday.'

'Oh. I'm so sorry for your loss.' He knew how Arthur must feel right now. He'd lost his wife. Had had to bury her. But *he'd* only had a few years with his wife. Arthur had had sixty-three years of marriage. He couldn't possibly imagine the level of loneliness the old man must be feeling.

'It was expected. The stroke took a lot out of her, I think.' Arthur cleared his throat and wiped his nose with the proper handkerchief he'd drawn from his jacket pocket. 'But I just wanted to say thank you for giving me a few extra days with her. They were important, all those minutes and hours we had, because she was sometimes lucid.'

'She was?'

Arthur nodded, smiling. 'Not for the entire time, but here and there—over the two days... You gave me back my wife. The stroke should have done her in, but you doctors—all your medicine, all your technology—gave her back to me. Just for a little while. I'd been afraid of her being lucid again. She'd been so upset the last time, discovering what was happening to her, but after the stroke it was like she came back to say goodbye. And that was precious to me, Dr Galloway.'

Matt gave a smile, but it was tinged with a resolute sadness.

'You never know how long you'll get with your loved ones on this planet, but when it comes to the end it's never enough, don't you think? We spend so much of life worrying about what other people think, what other people say, but when it comes to your final days is that what you worry about? Is that the most important thing? No, it's not. It's being with those you love. And if you're lucky enough to love, you embrace it. That's what Patty and I had in those final days. Love. And I needed to come here today to thank you for that.'

Arthur's words sank deep into Matt's soul.

He was right. The old guy was *right!* All the petty

day-to-day worries that he'd allowed to fester away in his skull meant nothing when he thought about it. If he was on his deathbed right now would he be worrying about what everyone thought of his feelings for Brooke? *No!* He'd want to be lying there holding her hand. Telling her how much he loved her! And knowing that she loved him!

Who were other people to judge when he should love again? Why was he allowing guilt to determine his feelings for her? Because, looking at himself right now, he saw that guilt was making him feel damned miserable! And who wanted to be miserable? When he was with Brooke he felt joy and contentment and happiness. Why couldn't he have that? Why couldn't *they?*

It didn't diminish the love he'd had for Jen. Not by one iota. And if other people thought that it did, then that was *their* issue.

Love—true love—was rare and beautiful, and if you were lucky enough to discover it you should embrace it, as Arthur had said. Not hide from it, nor feel guilty for having it. And there wasn't a clock or a timer on love. It could spring from anywhere. Unexpected and surprising. And didn't that make it all the more special?

'Thank you, Arthur. For coming here today. I really appreciate it.'

'Well, we appreciated *you*, Doc. That's it, really. I don't want to keep you. I know you're busy. Saving lives.'

Arthur was right. He had to save his *own* life. Because for the last few days he'd been drowning in guilt and grief and dying inside. *No more!*

He shook Arthur's outstretched hand and watched him go, and then he hurried off to find Brooke. He had to tell her everything. And if he hadn't messed it up too much he could be about to change both their lives.

* * *

It was hard to concentrate. Handing in her notice, know-ing she was pregnant a second time and still not in a solid relationship, weighed heavily. But Brooke did her best. No matter what was going on in her personal life, she still had to put her patients first.

She was good at that. Putting other people before her-self. It was something she'd had to do as a child and she'd chosen it as a profession. But though it usually brought her joy and satisfaction she felt no happiness today.

For her, contentment was a long way away, and she knew she would have to travel many a mile—both men-tally and geographically—before she found her happy place.

Her current patient should not even be in A&E. He had only come here because he couldn't get an appointment at his GP for another three weeks and he was concerned about a pain that he kept getting in his knee.

She did her best. She examined the knee. Couldn't see or feel anything wrong with it. Her patient could put weight on it, and he had a full range of movement, but he kept getting 'a painful twinge' that would make him gasp out loud when it struck.

Brooke suspected he might possibly be developing arthritis. The man had it in his family history. So she wrote him a prescription for some painkillers and told him to see his GP if it got worse. There was nothing else she could do for him now.

Her patient left, grumbling under his breath about shoddy patient care, and though normally that would have angered her today she had no energy for it. She had no energy for anything. Since she'd fallen out with Matt it was as if the life had gone out of her. All her vim, all her pep, was gone.

'Brooke? I must speak with you!' Matt came barrelling down the small corridor like a man on a mission.

She turned away. 'I'm not retracting my notice, so please don't ask.'

It hurt that he wouldn't just let it be. Couldn't he accept the fact that she was walking away to save her heart? Her soul? It was painful to be here with him and not be able to wrap her arms around him freely and share his kisses. It hurt that he'd shown her what love between them could be like and then cruelly torn it away.

She tried to pick up her stride. To get back to the doctors' desk, write up her notes, and then see her next patient. Anything that would make him go away—because it hurt too much to have him here and not be allowed to love him.

'I'm not here about your notice. I'm here about you. And me.'

Brooke turned to look at him, despair written across her features. 'I really don't think there's anything left to say. You've made it clear how you feel about us.'

'*No!* I haven't!'

She almost flinched at his raised voice, and she looked about them and noticed that some people were listening in—Kelly from the cubicle she was in, applying a splint; Michael the senior nurse, who was restocking a trolley, and further away the healthcare assistant, Michelle, who was bringing in a pile of blankets.

Feeling her cheeks colour, and not used to being the centre of everyone's attention, she glared at him. 'Keep your voice down.'

He lifted his chin. 'I will not. I don't care who hears. In fact, they all need to hear it.'

'Hear what?'

'That I love you, Dr Brooke Bailey. I'm in love with you and I will *always* be in love with you.'

Brooke swallowed. 'What?'

'I made a mistake. I'm human. I'm fallible. I panicked when I realised just how much you were coming to mean to me.'

'Matt—'

'I know I hurt you. It was never my intention.' He made her lock eyes with his. 'That New Zealand job... It was a dream that Jen and I once had. For Lily. Since Jen died I've tried to do everything in my power to make sure that Lily will know who her mother was. I put her in the crèche that Jen would have taken her to. I took her to the classes she signed her up for, and I took her job, so that Lily would know the place and the people who shared her mother's life. I rock her to sleep at night, telling her stories about her mother. And then I met you.'

Brooke could see there were tears in his eyes, and it made her feel like crying too.

'You were like a cyclone in my ordered world. You were at the crèche. You were here at work, and even at home. When I was alone my thoughts were of you. And after that night we spent together—'

Brooke blushed.

'I didn't know what to think. I felt guilty, yes. Not for what we did. What we had was beautiful and magical and perfect, and I've never felt that way with anyone. But I felt guilty for the fact that I wanted to stay with you. Stay in your flat and never leave. Take every part of you that you might offer. I forgot Jen for a few hours. And that made me feel so...'

He couldn't find the word he wanted.

'I had to soak up my old life. Remind myself of what I thought was important. What other people would expect of me. To be the grieving widower. To show respect—to take years, not months, before I fell in love with another woman. But feeling like I've lost you has almost killed me. I've been miserable. Ask anyone—they'll tell you. Lily's kept me going, as she did before, but she shouldn't have to be my crutch. Like you were for your father. I want her to feel loved and celebrated and valued and cherished—the way that I...I feel for you. You kept telling me I was honourable and brave but I didn't believe it. I've only just begun to believe that I am, and I feel that way, because of *you*. I love you, Brooke, and I want us to be together. You and me. For ever.'

Tears trickled down her cheeks as she heard his words. They were *real*. Heartfelt. Honest. And all around them the staff were smiling. Waiting for her reaction. She looked down, saw his hands. His wedding band was gone.

'You let me down, Matt.'

'I know. But if you just let me love you I promise, on my life, that it will never happen again.'

'I want to believe you. I *do*.'

'Then take a chance on us.'

She took in a breath. Then another. Tried to steady her frazzled nerves. 'I want to, but I'm scared.'

He stepped forward and took her hands in his. 'So am I. But that's okay, because I think we're *meant* to be scared. Nothing worth having is ever risk-free, but I think if we're scared *together* then we can face anything that life throws at us.'

She looked down at their hands, stroked the pale stripe on his finger where his wedding band had used to sit. 'Life has thrown a lot at us, hasn't it?'

He squeezed her fingers in response. 'It has.'

She looked up into his eyes. Those beautiful blue eyes that she knew so well and saw in her dreams. Wasn't this what she wanted? His love? And he'd announced it to everyone! No hiding. No shame. He had admitted his feelings for her in front of them all. All she had to do was be brave enough to accept it.

He was speaking again. 'A wise man told me recently that all that matters in this world is love. That if you have it you should embrace it, tell the person who's your everything that you love them. Because at the end of the day—at the end of life—that's all any of us ever want to say. I want to tell you I love you every day, Brooke Bailey. Every *single* day.'

A hesitant smile lifted the corners of her mouth. Reached her eyes. It was as if lights were slowly being turned on inside her, and she could feel warmth filling her once again as she opened herself up to the possibility that everything was about to turn out all right.

'I love you, Major Matthew Galloway.'

He smiled, joy lighting his eyes. 'You do?'

She nodded.

'Then let's be together. For ever.'

He lifted her hands to his lips and kissed the backs of her fingers, one after the other, and then pulled her close and kissed her properly.

Brooke sank into his embrace, feeling as if all the missing pieces of her puzzle were found. She was complete. Whole. It was terrifying, yes, but they would face the fear of this journey together.

Being back in his arms felt wonderful. It was soothing to her frazzled and exhausted body, and just by pressing up against him she could feel her energy returning. As if he was recharging her spent batteries with the depth of his emotion. His embrace, his touch, was everything. And she would never have to be without it again.

'There's one more thing,' she said.

He pulled back, looked at her. 'What is it?'

She lowered her voice so that only he could hear it. 'I'm pregnant.'

His eyes widened in surprise and then, barely milliseconds later, he lifted her off her feet and began swinging her around in happiness.

Brooke squealed and laughed and begged him to put her down—which he did.

'You're pregnant? That's amazing!'

'It's still early days. Anything could happen.'

He nodded. 'But we'll face it together.' He linked his hand into hers. 'Have I told you today that I love you?'

She smiled. 'Once or twice.'

'Well, I do. I do, I do, I *do*.'

'Well, Major, that's a good thing. Because I love you, too.'

They fell back into each other's arms, and all around everyone who knew them smiled with happiness.

There was no judgement.

Just joy.

For them.

As there always would be.

* * * * *

*If you enjoyed this story check out these
other great reads from Louisa Heaton*

*REUNITED BY THEIR PREGNANCY SURPRISE
CHRISTMAS WITH THE SINGLE DAD
SEVEN NIGHTS WITH HER EX
ONE LIFE-CHANGING NIGHT*

All available now!

MILLS & BOON®
Hardback – July 2017

ROMANCE

The Pregnant Kavakos Bride	Sharon Kendrick
The Billionaire's Secret Princess	Caitlin Crews
Sicilian's Baby of Shame	Carol Marinelli
The Secret Kept from the Greek	Susan Stephens
A Ring to Secure His Crown	Kim Lawrence
Wedding Night with Her Enemy	Melanie Milburne
Salazar's One-Night Heir	Jennifer Hayward
Claiming His Convenient Fiancée	Natalie Anderson
The Mysterious Italian Houseguest	Scarlet Wilson
Bound to Her Greek Billionaire	Rebecca Winters
Their Baby Surprise	Katrina Cudmore
The Marriage of Inconvenience	Nina Singh
The Surrogate's Unexpected Miracle	Alison Roberts
Convenient Marriage, Surprise Twins	Amy Ruttan
The Doctor's Secret Son	Janice Lynn
Reforming the Playboy	Karin Baine
Their Double Baby Gift	Louisa Heaton
Saving Baby Amy	Annie Claydon
The Baby Favour	Andrea Laurence
Lone Star Baby Scandal	Lauren Canan

MILLS & BOON®
Large Print – July 2017

ROMANCE

Secrets of a Billionaire's Mistress	Sharon Kendrick
Claimed for the De Carrillo Twins	Abby Green
The Innocent's Secret Baby	Carol Marinelli
The Temporary Mrs Marchetti	Melanie Milburne
A Debt Paid in the Marriage Bed	Jennifer Hayward
The Sicilian's Defiant Virgin	Susan Stephens
Pursued by the Desert Prince	Dani Collins
Return of Her Italian Duke	Rebecca Winters
The Millionaire's Royal Rescue	Jennifer Faye
Proposal for the Wedding Planner	Sophie Pembroke
A Bride for the Brooding Boss	Bella Bucannon

HISTORICAL

Surrender to the Marquess	Louise Allen
Heiress on the Run	Laura Martin
Convenient Proposal to the Lady	Julia Justiss
Waltzing with the Earl	Catherine Tinley
At the Warrior's Mercy	Denise Lynn

MEDICAL

Falling for Her Wounded Hero	Marion Lennox
The Surgeon's Baby Surprise	Charlotte Hawkes
Santiago's Convenient Fiancée	Annie O'Neil
Alejandro's Sexy Secret	Amy Ruttan
The Doctor's Diamond Proposal	Annie Claydon
Weekend with the Best Man	Leah Martyn

0617 GEN STD LP

MILLS & BOON®
Hardback – August 2017

ROMANCE

An Heir Made in the Marriage Bed	Anne Mather
The Prince's Stolen Virgin	Maisey Yates
Protecting His Defiant Innocent	Michelle Smart
Pregnant at Acosta's Demand	Maya Blake
The Secret He Must Claim	Chantelle Shaw
Carrying the Spaniard's Child	Jennie Lucas
A Ring for the Greek's Baby	Melanie Milburne
Bought for the Billionaire's Revenge	Clare Connelly
The Runaway Bride and the Billionaire	Kate Hardy
The Boss's Fake Fiancée	Susan Meier
The Millionaire's Redemption	Therese Beharrie
Captivated by the Enigmatic Tycoon	Bella Bucannon
Tempted by the Bridesmaid	Annie O'Neil
Claiming His Pregnant Princess	Annie O'Neil
A Miracle for the Baby Doctor	Meredith Webber
Stolen Kisses with Her Boss	Susan Carlisle
Encounter with a Commanding Officer	Charlotte Hawkes
Rebel Doc on Her Doorstep	Lucy Ryder
The CEO's Nanny Affair	Joss Wood
Tempted by the Wrong Twin	Rachel Bailey

MILLS & BOON®
Large Print – August 2017

ROMANCE

The Italian's One-Night Baby	Lynne Graham
The Desert King's Captive Bride	Annie West
Once a Moretti Wife	Michelle Smart
The Boss's Nine-Month Negotiation	Maya Blake
The Secret Heir of Alazar	Kate Hewitt
Crowned for the Drakon Legacy	Tara Pammi
His Mistress with Two Secrets	Dani Collins
Stranded with the Secret Billionaire	Marion Lennox
Reunited by a Baby Bombshell	Barbara Hannay
The Spanish Tycoon's Takeover	Michelle Douglas
Miss Prim and the Maverick Millionaire	Nina Singh

HISTORICAL

Claiming His Desert Princess	Marguerite Kaye
Bound by Their Secret Passion	Diane Gaston
The Wallflower Duchess	Liz Tyner
Captive of the Viking	Juliet Landon
The Spaniard's Innocent Maiden	Greta Gilbert

MEDICAL

Their Meant-to-Be Baby	Caroline Anderson
A Mummy for His Baby	Molly Evans
Rafael's One Night Bombshell	Tina Beckett
Dante's Shock Proposal	Amalie Berlin
A Forever Family for the Army Doc	Meredith Webber
The Nurse and the Single Dad	Dianne Drake

MILLS & BOON®

Why shop at millsandboon.co.uk?

Each year, thousands of romance readers find their perfect read at millsandboon.co.uk. That's because we're passionate about bringing you the very best romantic fiction. Here are some of the advantages of shopping at www.millsandboon.co.uk:

* **Get new books first**—you'll be able to buy your favourite books one month before they hit the shops

* **Get exclusive discounts**—you'll also be able to buy our specially created monthly collections, with up to 50% off the RRP

* **Find your favourite authors**—latest news, interviews and new releases for all your favourite authors and series on our website, plus ideas for what to try next

* **Join in**—once you've bought your favourite books, don't forget to register with us to rate, review and join in the discussions

Visit **www.millsandboon.co.uk**
for all this and more today!